CW01502326

BEARQUAKE

Created by
David Griffiths & James Leader

Novelisation by
David Griffiths

ISBN-13: 978-1536827217

Copyright © 2016 David Griffiths
All rights reserved.

No part of this publication may be reproduced, stored in a
retrieval system, or transmitted, in any form or by any means,
electronic, mechanical, photocopying, recording or otherwise,
without the prior written permission of the author.

This is a work of fiction. Names, characters, businesses, places,
events and incidents are either the products of the author's
imagination or used in a fictitious manner. Any resemblance to
actual persons, living or dead, or actual events is purely
coincidental.

No bears were harmed in the telling of this story.

By the same author

A Christmas Cthulhu
Maelstrom (illustrated by Jon Lon)

Praise for David Griffiths

"Packed with laugh out loud moments... A tightly written drama...Well-observed dialogue by David Griffiths...An unmistakeably authentic ring." *Liverpool Echo*

"A triumph" *Liverpool Daily Post*

"Sharp, well-timed dialogue" *Three Weeks, Edinburgh*

"Brilliantly scripted...It's impossible to fault a play that's conceived and brought about with such sophistication." *Fringe Guru*

"So many twists you won't be able to put it down." *Amazon Reviewer*

For Vicki

CONTENTS

CHAPTER 1

The signs dotted around the campsite asked all campers to keep noise to a minimum during the night. But the thumping music and drunken cheers rendered the signs ineffective. At any other time of year, this may have resulted in a visit from the Park Rangers, but this was the first day of Spring Break and the Rangers knew better than to try and control the young partygoers who were currently occupying the Park.

Like so many National Parks the site was huge, and the revellers occupied a significant portion of the campsites. They sat, huddled around campfires laughing, singing and drinking.

From the trees, the campsites glowed with activity. In the centre the bonfires burnt, illuminating the surrounding tents. The silhouettes of teenagers staggered drunkenly between the tents carrying bottles of beer. The smoke of the campfire mingled with the exhale of tobacco and marijuana.

A stereo was cranked to its highest volume, to drown out the fumbling grunts of drunken sex in a nearby tent. As the music began to thump, a small group jumped to their feet and began to dance.

Aimee sat near the fire, grinning at her friends. She took a gulp of beer as she turned back to the comfort of the flames.

Among the dancers were her boyfriend Nick, his best friend Jake and Lisa – a recent addition to their group. Lisa was normally much more reserved, but she stood dancing and grinding next to Jake. Aimee couldn't help but grin. Spring Break was bringing out the party animal in Lisa.

Nick was feeling the effects of the alcohol. It didn't take him long to rejoin his girlfriend by the fire. They shared a quick kiss before they realised they had been joined by Jake and Lisa.

'Spring break, you guys.' Lisa grinned.

Aimee raised her beer bottle. 'It's awesome to get out of the city for a few days. Felt like I was gonna snap.' She had lived her life in small towns, surrounded by farming communities. As much as she enjoyed the city, it never felt like home. But around the campfire, Aimee was far more relaxed.

'My Dad thinks I'm studying,' Lisa offered, conspiratorially before letting out a guffaw.

'All holiday?'

'Why not? He'd freak out if he saw me here.'

Jake gave her a playful dig. 'You *are* studying. Have you seen the geysers in this Park? They're incredible.'

Lisa shrugged, 'Yeah, maybe I'm studying Geology.'

Aimee had to ask. 'What are you Majoring?'

'Politics.'

The group let out a laugh, then swallowed down another bottle of beer each. Nick looked around the campfire for a cooler. There was no beer to hand. 'Another?' he asked Aimee, who nodded. He staggered to his feet as Jake eyed Lisa.

'Help me carry some beer back, dude.'

Jake looked frustrated, his blossoming romance interrupted by his friend. He rose and followed Nick to the tent, all the while glancing back at Lisa.

Aimee positioned herself next to Lisa.

'So, you two.'

'What?'

Aimee grinned, 'You know.'

Lisa gave a derisory roll of her eyes, 'Oh, please.'

'Why not? I think you make a cute couple.'

Unable to hide her smile, Lisa blushed. 'Well, he is kinda hot.'

Aimee laughed.

On the opposite end of the camp, Nick helped himself to a pack of beer before nudging his friend. 'Just go for it, man.'

'I dunno, Nick,' Jake took a lot longer to lose his inhibitions than Nick. That had always been the way. 'What if she's not interested?'

Nick handed him a beer. 'So what, dude? So she's not interested and you find that out. Means you don't spend the rest of Spring Break moping, am I right?'

Jake paused, weighing it up in his head. Begrudgingly, he agreed.

'So go for it.'

With a quick roll of his eyes, Jake nodded the affirmative. Nick held his can out in front of his friend and they clinked cans.

As the night wore on, the party continued. As the teenagers became drunker, the music became gradually louder. The occasional couple would break away, retiring to tents or finding a secluded corner of the surrounding woods. Through it all, Aimee's group had sat talking and joking around the fire. Jake and Lisa drew closer together whilst Aimee had playfully suggested a drinking game, which had prompted Nick to break out a bottle of Tequila. They sat with their umpteenth shot spilling in their laps as they rocked drunkenly.

'OK, my turn,' Aimee laughed, 'I have never… cheated on a test.'

Nick shrugged and took a drink. 'That was pretty lame.' He took his time, considering all options before offering with a wry smile, 'I have never made out with the same sex.'

There was a pause. Aimee then took an embarrassed drink, much to the delight of her boyfriend.

'No way! That is awesome!'

Nick turned to high five his friend, but found Jake indisposed. Having given up on the game entirely, Jake was kissing Lisa – both oblivious to the party that was continuing around them. As happy as he was to see his friend get the girl, Nick couldn't shake the revelation his girlfriend had just told him. 'It was no big deal,' Aimee shrugged it off.

'No big deal? You know how many men would

kill for a girlfriend like you?'

Aimee knew that Nick was joking, but even so, it felt an oddly romantic thing to say. For a moment, she couldn't say anything. Then regaining her composure, she sought to continue the game.

'I have never had sex with someone over forty.'

To her surprise, Nick took a proud drink of his beer. 'Seriously?'

Nick laughed. 'Let's just say I was schooled in the ways of love.'

Far from the party, near the entrance to the Park, Hank Walker fished a packet of cigarettes from his jacket pocket. At his age, he was resigned to the fact that they would probably kill him. But he was too long in the tooth to quit. His wife insisted he try, which was why he had taken to only smoking at work. The long days and nights certainly helped feed his habit.

Besides, he needed something to keep him calm. The upcoming weekend would be long and arduous for his team of Rangers. Spring Break had already seen a huge number of visitors to the Park, but tomorrow Hunting Season would begin. And having hundreds of hippy college kids and a bunch of gun-toting hicks in the same Park at the same time just gave Hank a headache.

From the porch of the Ranger Station, he looked in to the pitch black forest as he lit his cigarette and took a drag.

'Promised your wife I'd help you quit.'

The voice came from the doorway of the Station. Deputy Kevin Payton, a young man, stood leaning against the door frame. They had worked together for a number of years. Hank trusted Kevin, he knew that Kevin would likely take over from him once he retired. He'd schooled Kevin in running the Park and his family had taken a shine to him. Kevin had become like a son.

Hank exhaled, a cloud of smoke dissipating in the night. He smiled to his Deputy, defiantly.

'She was pretty insistent.'

'I hear that.'

Kevin was by the book. Hank appreciated that, but it also meant that he'd come down hard on the rules. And if Mrs Walker had given him an instruction, he'd be sure to follow it to the letter. It was equally admirable and damned frustrating.

After a few more uncomfortable drags, Hank could bear Kevin's disapproval no longer. He took the cigarette from his mouth and stomped it out with his boot.

'All right. Happy?'

But Kevin was unmoved.

'Something else, Deputy?'

Hank watched for a moment, then Kevin disappeared back in to the doorway and reappeared momentarily with a trash can. He held it out to the Sheriff, who sighed. Hank picked up the discarded cigarette butt and threw it in to the trash can, hoping that this would placate his young Deputy.

It didn't.

'Aw, Christ.'

Reaching in to his jacket pocket, Hank pulled out the open packet of cigarettes. Kevin was unmoved in the stand-off between cigarettes and trash can. Hank relented, throwing the packet in the trash.

Satisfied, Kevin looked to the clear night sky. The stars were magnificent and bright. The forest buffered the sound of the drunken revelry. From the Ranger Station, all was peaceful.

'Quiet night, huh,' Kevin offered as an icebreaker.

Hank nodded. 'Enjoy the peace while it lasts.'

'Wonder if them bears know what's in store for 'em.'

Hank was no fan of hunting season, but as Ranger it was his job to coordinate. The Mayor would salivate over the amount of traffic in town, the trade, the taxes. It was their most lucrative season. The bear population was in for its annual cull, regardless of numbers, all for the good of the Almighty Dollar.

'If I were them, I'd stay in their caves. Don't know what'd piss me off more - the asshole spring breakers or the asshole hunters.'

Kevin nodded, 'Circle of Life, I guess.'

But the thought of the hunt was starting to irritate Hank, as it did every year. It wasn't just the killing – he knew his daughter, Sophie, would be down here with her protester friends. It put him in an even more awkward position and it pissed him off.

'Ain't it funny how we always put it down to 'Circle of Life', providing we're on top of the food chain? Minute something were to start hunting for us, then we'd have to look at things differently.' Hank was just letting off steam.

'Sheriff?' Kevin was concerned.

Hank waved him off, 'Ah, I'm just tired.'

He stepped down from the porch and strode toward his Jeep that was parked upon the path. I'm gonna get some shut eye. I'll see you first thing, all right?'

'Good night, Hank.'

From inside the tent, Aimee was aware just how much noise could be heard from outside. Her senses heightened, she fumbled under the sleeping bag as quietly as she could. But the occasional moan of pleasure from Nick only served to draw further attention to their withdrawal from the party.

They kissed as Aimee repositioned herself on top of her boyfriend, reaching down and taking him in her hand and guiding him inside her.

There was no longer any way to disguise what they were doing. She was pretty sure that the tent had started to sway and couldn't help but think how comical it may look to any passers by.

Caught up in the moment, she pulled the zip back on the sleeping bag, and sat up astride Nick. She arched her back as she fell in to a rhythm.

'What happened to Jake and Lisa?' Nick asked. Perhaps not the best time to enquire, but Nick wanted to be sure that his friend was enjoying his night as much as he was.

'I saw them slink off an hour ago,' Aimee offered through her gasps.

Nick beamed, 'Way to go, buddy.'

Aimee stopped, leaning in to steal back Nick's focus. 'Less about those two. We've got our own fun right here.' She took Nick's hands, placing them upon her breasts. Her nipples were instantly hard.

She began to grind harder, Nick moaning his approval.

There was a sudden slow rumble, the tent shook and Aimee was aware just how obvious this now looked. But she no longer cared. She was enjoying the moment. Let people see them.

The tent shook again, the rumbling more evident, more violent.

'What the hell was that?' Nick asked.

Ignoring it, Aimee leaned in to kiss Nick .

In the following tremor, Aimee lost her balance and was thrown to the ground violently.

Having crept away from Aimee's drinking games a few hours ago, Jake and Lisa had playfully chased each other to a secluded spot far from the crowded campsite. They had sat together for over an hour, occasionally talking, mostly kissing. But their passion had overcome them. They now lay amongst the leaves, Lisa staring up in to the deep night sky as Jake thrust on top of her. A drunken fumble in the most tranquil of spots, both of them caught up in the moment, their breathing heavy and their immediate lust for each other almost satiated.

With a final thrust, Jake let out an orgasmic cry and Lisa drew him in for a passionate kiss. Their foreheads met as they gazed longingly in to each other's eyes. And just as their lovemaking subsided, they felt a tremor in the earth. A deep vibration that further stimulated Lisa, who let out a squeal of approval.

Jake just smiled at his lover, 'Did the Earth just move?'

The Sheriff now long gone, Kevin sat with his feet up on his desk with a book in his hand. He enjoyed the night shift, usually peaceful, the occasional call from a campsite. But ultimately, it was a time to catch up on his reading, sat in the log cabin with some soft lighting and a log fire burning.

The first tremor went unnoticed.

The second rattled the contents of Kevin's desk. Thinking that a vehicle had pulled up outside, Kevin rose and crossed to the window. He peered out. Nothing.

Kevin started as the following tremor rocked the cabin, throwing frames from the walls and shattering glass across the floor. Crossing to his desk, he tried to secure the contents as the earthquake forced the desk in to a dance across the floorboards. In the corner the bookcase tipped, spilling books upon the floor. The filing cabinets rattled open.

As suddenly as it had started, the tremors stopped.

The long drive out of the park was unlit. The headlights of Hank's Jeep shone full beam as he cautiously navigated the road.

A few hours sleep and he'd be due back for the official Park opening ceremony for the season. Sadly as Sheriff, he would be expected there. Retirement couldn't come any sooner.

The car bounced, the smooth country road broken up.

Hank's brow furrowed. Had he hit something? The car had shaken…

He glanced in his mirror, squinting in to the black.

Nothing.

His eyes darted back to the road ahead. 'Shit!' Hank slammed the brakes and the Jeep screeched to a halt.

Ahead, the tarmac writhed and contorted.

As the ground shook, a tree was uprooted and began a slow creaking descent towards the hood of the car. Thinking fast, Hank threw the Jeep in to reverse and pulled free just in time. The tree crumpled on to the road in front of him.

Pulling his shorts up to his waist, Nick scrambled to the door of the tent and unzipped it. Sticking his head through the gap, he surveyed the camp.

Tents had collapsed, fires had extinguished, tent poles were bent or had snapped completely. From the fallen tents, students crawled out from under the tarpaulin. More than anything, Nick noticed that the music had stopped.

'That must have been some 'quake,' said Aimee from the tent.

She was right.

It was enough of a 'quake to end the party.

Lisa pulled her clothes around her as she dressed on the grass. Stood staring in to the distance, Jake buttoned his jeans. He stopped, alerted to something in the trees. Whatever it was, Lisa was suddenly hit with fear. Her hands shook as she struggled in to her remaining clothes.

'What's up?'

'Thought I heard something.'

Lisa jumped to her feet and half laughed, nervously. 'Other than an earthquake?'

But Jake hushed her, which only made her more nervous. 'I dunno. Sounded like an animal, or...' He trailed off as he listened closely. Lisa couldn't hear anything. Was Jake just trying to scare her?

She scoffed, 'Probably just Nick trying to freak you out.'

'Could be a dog.'

Had they seen any dogs at camp? She wondered.

Jake slowly edged closer to the trees, staring intently into the darkness. Lisa could make out a shadow, perhaps that of a boulder. It looked like a rock, round and unmoving.

And Jake moved in closer.

A faint snort, Jake raised his hands slowly, defensively.

He whispered; 'There's something over here.'

Lisa began to panic, her heart fluttering, her voice trembling. 'Let's just get back to camp, see if our tent's still standing.' She wanted to run, wanted to scream. But would she look completely ridiculous? It was probably nothing. Or a prank. Most likely a prank. Some pervert who'd been watching them all this time.

Drawn to the sound, Jake pushed back some branches and slowly crept towards the sound.

'Jake.'

He was swallowed up by the forest. Invisible. Lisa was visibly shaking. She was now alone. Slowly, she moved towards where Jake had disappeared.

There was a howl.

Straight ahead. Not an animal, but a human, screaming out as if startled. The bushes rustled violently, tree branches creaked and snapped. Lisa held her breath, not knowing what to say or do.

Then they were still.

Her fear giving way to anger, Lisa screamed out, 'Jake? Stop screwing around. Asshole!'

Jake did not respond.

Another rustle and an object rolled out from the bushes, bouncing along the grass and stopping at Lisa's feet. It looked like a ball. Furious, she shouted, 'You want to play? Fine, we'll play back at the camp. Are you coming?'

Silence.

Did she even know her way back? She was beginning to doubt herself, but she couldn't let her fear show. Not now.

She reached down. 'Then I guess I'll just take this ball and...'

Lisa was frozen to the spot.

The ball was wet and warm.

It was Jake's head, frozen in a scream.

Lisa tried to scream, but it was too late.

It bounded through the trees, its eyes glowing red, mouth dripping with blood.

Too late.

CHAPTER 2

Hank had spent most of the morning coordinating his Rangers in the removal of felled trees that blocked the road in to the Park. The tarmac was cracked, in need of some serious repair. It couldn't have happened on a worse day. But there was nothing that could be done about it today. He resigned himself to the task at hand and within a few hours the path was reasonably clear and the Ranger Station was mid decoration for the celebration.

The Mayor was running late, which meant that Hank would have to contend with the Press himself should any awkward questions be asked prior to the opening ceremony.

The Production Trucks arrived just before noon, the Reporters gathering near the cabin's porch. They were followed shortly after by the first wave of tourists, campers and hunters – a queue of trailers and RVs stretched back to the Highway.

Hank tied off the 'Welcome' banner above the Ranger Station as Kevin wrapped the last of the bunting around the beams. As Hank strode back towards his office, the Reporters surrounded him.

'Hank, Hank, what's the word on last night's 'quake?' He knew them all personally. Local crews, covered most of the Park's major events. They didn't bother him all that much, but there was still a lot of preparation that needed to be done.

'Is the area unstable? How will this affect the season?'

Hank tried to push through the small crowd. 'Give me a break, huh fellas? Is a 'quake really that unusual in this part of the world?' He hoped this would placate them. Personally, he wanted to ensure that the Park was safe before any more people took up residence.

'How about rumours that the Mayor is to close the Park as a public safety precaution?'

'The Mayor doesn't interfere in our operation.' This was a lie. He knew the Mayor would want the Park open at all costs. He wouldn't listen to Hank.

'He's waiting for you inside, Hank.' How had he missed him? Too busy getting the place in order. Mayor Bob must have crept in unannounced. It hadn't gone unnoticed by the Press, but Hank knew he'd be waiting (and seething) in Hank's Office.

With a final push, he freed himself from the reporters and fought his way to the door. Holding the door as he entered, he forced it shut before the reporters could block it. They knocked on the glass of the door, but Hank closed the blind. With a sigh of relief, he stepped in to reception.

'Kevin?' he shouted.

His Deputy was nowhere to be seen. Crossing the hallway, Hank was stopped by a young student, who emerged from a vacant office.

'Sheriff Walker.' Lori Esposito seemed in a hurry to speak to him. The young Puerto Rican certainly commanded his attention, her figure was certainly enough to stop Hank in his tracks. Of course, Lori was young enough to be his daughter, but she was beautiful.

'Oh, hey Lori. You seen Kevin?'

Lori had occupied an office at the Ranger Station for the semester. A seismology student, she had found herself staying on for longer than expected. The Rangers liked having the extra company and the Park proved an excellent base of operations for her to work on her paper.

'I think he's out back.' Lori had seen Kevin pass her earlier. But she had something far more important to discuss. 'I think you need to see the readings from last night's earthquake.'

Hank was too busy, he waved her off. 'Lori, you're the Seismology Major, not me. I just let you use the office.' He continued to the kitchen, picked up the pot of filter coffee and poured himself a mug. Lori followed him.

'The results are quite interesting.'

It wouldn't be the first time that Lori had tried to explain her findings to Hank. He was no scientist. The last thing he needed on his busiest day of the season was a science lesson.

'Why is everyone so obsessed with this earthquake? You know, a tree narrowly missed the Jeep last night. That's as bad as things got.' He was getting increasingly tetchy. He felt around his breast pocket for his cigarettes and remembered that Kevin had confiscated them last night. He took a gulp of coffee to calm himself down, but Lori continued.

'That's last night's earthquake.' She held a chart up for him to see. It showed a significant spike, but Hank had very little idea of what that actually meant. 'I've checked my readings against the United States Geological Survey and they compare. A 6.2 Magnitude earthquake. That's huge. That's the force you could expect from a nuclear explosion, and then some.'

Admittedly, that sounded impressive. Hank raised his eyebrows, surprised. He needed those cigarettes. 'Sure didn't feel that big.'

'The Moment Magnitude is a measure of the slip on the fault. It doesn't really measure the feel of the earthquake on the surface. For a major metropolitan area, this could have been pretty devastating. But for parkland, heavy soil density...'

'English please, Lori.'

'A park doesn't shake like a skyscraper. It's not designed to withstand. Nature is unpredictable.'

He understood her meaning. The Park was not safe. He needed to ensure full precautions were met. Were all their campers accounted for? Had his Rangers performed a head count this morning?

Hank took a sip of his coffee and offered, matter-of-factly, 'So, we had a bad earthquake.'

Lori was grinning from ear to ear. It was the happiest Hank had seen her since she arrived at the Park. She was starting to enjoy herself. 'We sure did. Never seen one like it.'

Her enthusiasm couldn't help but make Hank smile. 'Look at you. You're enjoying this. Who'd have thought your assignment could be fun, huh? What was it you called us again?'

Embarrassed, Lori muttered, 'I can't remember.'

Hank did. 'God fearing redneck hillbillies, wasn't it?'

Lori hung her head. 'I may have exaggerated.'

'You got that right.'

Hank began to search through the trash cans, looking for his cigarettes that Kevin confiscated the night before. Lori followed him. 'Can you blame me? My classmates travelled to Australia. This place is beautiful, but it's no Australia.'

Gone. Kevin had probably taken them with him, to insure against relapse. 'And how many of them are reading a force 6 on the Richter Scale?'

She corrected him; 'Moment Magnitude Scale. Richter hasn't been used since the seventies - except in movies.'

Hank leaned against the counter and raised his coffee mug to Lori, triumphantly. 'Congratulations.' He finished his mug, placed it on to the counter and marched towards his office. He could see the silhouette of a figure sat at his desk. Mayor Bob was waiting.

Lori gave chase. 'That's not all.'

Hank stopped and sighed. 'Lori, can this wait a couple days? We've got thousands of hunters ready to descend on this park today, hunting licences to confirm, the goddamn press to deal with, that's before we repair the roads from last night's tremor. Add to that all the drunken teenagers running around and you can appreciate...'

Lori cut him off. 'The seismograph shows another tremor that took place shortly after the first.'

Hank paused.

'An aftershock?'

'That's what I thought at first. An aftershock or some kind of echo, but the readings are far too different.'

Hank thought logically. 'We had two separate 'quakes.'

'This park lies on a fault line,' Lori explained, 'You would expect any kind of tremor to give a clear signal, something defined. This second reading... it just doesn't look right. It's as if the first earthquake triggered something or started something in motion.'

Now Hank was paying attention. He had wanted to make sure the Park was clear before more tourists descended. But if there was a possibility of more...

He'd need something more concrete than this to take to Mayor Bob.

'You think we're in for worse?'

Lori scrambled through her notes. 'My estimate puts the second tremor a lot closer to the surface. It could be a landslide, the earth settling from such a large disturbance. Or it could be something forcing its way to the surface.'

'Like a geyser?' They were one of the Park's most popular tourist attractions, but also one of their most dangerous. Any further eruptions could cause serious injury. Even death.

'You've got plenty of geysers, Sheriff. They don't register like this. This was more like a crack in the tectonic plates, maybe some magma bursting through.'

He wanted to shout, but Hank spoke quietly, deliberately, discreetly. 'Woah, like what? Like a volcano?'

'Could be.'

Hank's jaw hung open. 'A dormant volcano.' The ramifications could be disastrous.

'That would be my best guess. I may need to call the University, get some experts out here to check my work, but that'd take a couple days.'

But Hank wasn't listening. All he could think of were the thousands of tourists descending on the park. There were campers here already, spread across the vast expanse of forest. 'We've got people out there.'

'I'm sorry, Sheriff. If I were you, I'd shut down for a few days. Just to be certain.'

Complete lock down, survey the land, make absolutely sure it's safe before reopening. But how would he convince Mayor Bob? Lori couldn't be wrong about this. Hank needed her to be absolutely sure. 'I can't tell the Mayor to shut this place down. Not without proof.'

Lori nodded, 'I was going to take a trip up to the geysers this morning, see if they can tell us anything. If there're any residual tremors, they're probably the best place to look.'

'I'll drive you up there. Let me just get my jacket.' If nothing else, it would be an excuse for Hank to remove himself from the media circus outside. Lori had hurried back to her office to hastily pack some equipment and Hank stepped in to his office, reaching for his jacket which hung near the door.

'Sheriff Walker, how are you?' Mayor Bob Brady

sat at Hank's desk. He had completely forgotten about his visitor. He was too caught up in talk of volcanoes and park closures. It dawned on Hank that he may need to have a conversation with Mayor Bob now – despite their need to gather further evidence. 'I hear you had quite the close call last night. Out on the road.'

Hank just nodded in greeting. 'Mr Mayor.'

Mayor Bob rose from Hank's desk. He crossed to him, hand outstretched, and Hank was acutely aware of how Bob had manipulated their encounter – the use of Hank's desk, putting him on the back foot, putting Mayor Bob in the position of authority. He just gritted his teeth.

'Damn fine day for a hunt, wouldn't you agree?' Mayor Bob seemed far more enthusiastic than normal. Was he playing politics or could Hank smell alcohol on his breath? 'Press Office suggested I come down here early, what with last night's touch of weather. We wanted our public to know they were in safe hands. Now, if we start by...'

Hank had to cut him off. 'Mr Mayor, there's a few things...'

'Oh, I appreciate you're busy, son. I wouldn't want to stand in your way. So if we just get this photo opportunity out of the way, we can all get back to business.'

They stood facing each other. Hank paused, looking for the words. If only he'd not come back for his jacket, he could have avoided this...

Mayor Bob frowned. 'Well hell, Walker, looks like you've just seen a ghost.'

'Mr Mayor, last night's earthquake...'

With a wave, Mayor Bob dismissed Hank's concerns, 'Oh, I don't want to hear about it. You know how many licences we've issued this season? Record numbers!' He was grinning with delight. Hank's determined expression unsettled him and his face darkened. 'I don't want nobody spooked by some earthquake.'

'That was no ordinary earthquake.'

CHAPTER 3

The queue of campers and RVs stretched back a few miles. The Greenbergs had been waiting patiently in their motor home. Rita had decided to make a pot of coffee whilst they waited and brought it back to Saul. Visiting the park was their latest stop on what Saul liked to describe as their 'Retirement Tour'. The kids had moved away, the business had been sold and Rita and Saul were finally content to live life for themselves. It had been a long time coming. In fact, this year marked their forty-fifth wedding anniversary. They were already making plans for their fiftieth, but Saul took the pragmatic approach of enjoying life whilst they could.

Who knew where they would be five years from now?

By the time they turned in to the park itself, Saul's coffee had gone cold. On their slow approach to the Reception area, they surveyed the countless trucks and jeeps. Rita rinsed the cups out in the kitchen as Saul sighed.

'What is it, Saul?' she shouted to her husband.

Saul watched intently as men unloaded large bags, cases and equipment from their trucks. Invariably, there were shotguns strapped to their backs. Saul imagined most of the hard cases contained small arsenals. It frustrated him. 'All these people, the needless slaughter of animals. I just don't understand it.'

Shrugging, Rita reassured her husband, 'They're bears, dear. They're a pest.'

'To who? The salmon?' Saul was frustrated. 'Whoever heard of a pest that hibernates all winter. That's some considerate pest.'

Rita was used to Saul's ranting. He was just tired from the drive, wanting to set up camp and stretch his legs. 'Well, if it makes them feel like big men.'

The RV continued to crawl along the approach to the Ranger's Station and Saul pointed accusingly out of the window at some passing hunters. 'And the size of those guns. I'd joke about them overcompensating, but it's no laughing matter. There are kids out here.'

They had spent so much of their lives living in the city, it had been Rita's idea to tour the countryside – to get in touch with nature. Saul was less enthusiastic with the rural lifestyle. But there was one thing that irked Saul more than hunting. After forty-five years, Rita knew how to push his buttons. She smirked as she said, 'We could go to Disneyland.'

'Disneyland?' Saul ranted, 'How does that put us in touch with nature? A giant mouse wearing a tuxedo?'

'Then just relax, Saul. Enough with the stress, already.' Rita stood over Saul and rubbed his shoulders. He was tense from the drive. Saul closed his eyes, leaned back and smiled.

'Ah, you've got the hands of an angel.'

She kissed him on the forehead, wrapping her arms around his neck. 'This trip was a wonderful idea, Saul.'

Saul smiled. Despite the gripes, he was having the time of his life. 'Some people retire and sit at home. Not us.'

As the RV pulled up outside the Ranger Station, Rita spotted a payphone through the crowd. She pointed, 'I can check in with the kids.'

'Kids? Rita, they're thirty seven and forty two.'

'I just haven't spoken to them all week.'

Saul kissed her hand. 'Let them worry about us. We chased them enough when they were teenagers. Besides, they bought us this motor home for us to enjoy it, not to tour the payphones of America.'

The motor home had been a retirement present. Encouragement for them to get active. It had been ideal, Rita admitted. 'You're right, dear. Let's find our lot and I'll make us another pot of coffee.'

As the Greenbergs parked up, a group of teenagers navigated the heavy footfall in front of the Ranger Station and began to form a group. All in their late teens, they dressed scruffy, wore their hair long and carried large placards. They congregated to a seventeen year old girl, their leader. She seemed much more mature than the rest and her knowledge of the park was evident as her eyes darted around, identifying camera crews and local rangers,

She spotted a reporter mid-broadcast and rallied her fellow protestors. Together, they herded behind him as he spoke live to his viewers.

'The start of Bear Season inevitably brings with it those who are against the hunt. Behind me, protestors are already amassing. Let's see if we can get a few words.' Turning the tables, the reporter thrust a microphone in to the face of the young girl leader. 'And who are you, miss?'

The girl spoke confidently. 'Sophie. Sophie Walker.'

'Can you tell our viewers what you're here for today?'

Eloquently, Sophie began, 'Well, I thought it was pretty obvious. The bear population in this park has declined dramatically in the past thirty years – a decline that can be linked exclusively to this unnecessary violence. It is our belief that the hunting of bears need not happen in our National Parks, in fact doing so will see bears endangered within a decade.'

'Surely hunting licences are limited to a certain number to help maintain the population?' the reporter offered. Sophie became irate.

'Maintain the population? This forest *belongs* to the bears. We need to spend less time screwing with their natural habitat and let nature take its course.' A cheer went up from her comrades behind her. She flashed them a smile. In the corner of her eye, she could see the deriding glances from the gathered hunters.

The reporter continued, 'And if the bear population gets too high? If they threaten campers? What then?'

Smug, Sophie decided to up her game. 'We lose a few morons with guns and some pot smoking teenagers. I'd say the bears were doing us a favour.' Having been deliberately provocative, Sophie turned away. The reporter stepped away from the crowd of protesters as he continued, 'There you have it. Back to the studio.'

Sophie laughed as a few of her group gave her a high five.

Having given Mayor Bob the full picture, Hank leaned back upon his desk waiting for his response. Mayor Bob looked grim. Hank knew he wouldn't go for it, but he needed to make him aware of the situation.

After a pause, Mayor Bob said, 'Son, there is no way I am closing this park on a busy weekend like this.'

Hardly unexpected. But Hank had to convince him. 'Give me a day. Just to be sure.'

Mayor Bob just laughed, incredulous. 'Are you crazy?'

'There could be lives in danger.'

Mayor Bob was starting to lose his cool. 'Idle speculation.' He pointed a finger threateningly at the Sheriff, his voice raised. 'You are gonna open them campsites like you do every year, you hear me?'

Hank could feel his heart rate increase, his adrenaline start to pump, his cheeks redden with anger. He thought about reaching out, grabbing the accusatory finger and snapping it in half. He could grab Mayor Bob by his fucking neck, make him close the park. Sure, he might lose his job, but what was it worth if people died as a result of some dumbass instruction from Bob Brady?

These thoughts spun around Hank's mind as he stood eye to eye with Mayor Bob, who dropped his hand to his side and puffed his chest out some more, 'Or do I have to appoint a new Park Sheriff? That Deputy of yours is mighty skilled.'

Fists clenched, jaw squared, veins rising on Hank's neck. He knew Mayor Bob was being provocative. Maybe he wanted Hank to punch him, would make replacing him a whole lot easier. He thought of his family – his wife and teenage daughter. As close to retirement as he was, could he afford to lose his job at this moment in time? His daughter would probably find it amusing, but he doubted his wife would approve. Taking a moment, Hank tried to calm down. Mayor Bob recognised this, it made him puff his chest out a little further. He had won. 'That's what I thought,' he said smugly.

Hank opened his office door, indicating for Mayor Bob to leave. He sauntered out, the face of public office – measured, reposed, friendly. Hank followed, slamming his office door as he did.

At Reception, two teenagers talked to Deputy Kevin. He recognised them as two of the spring breakers. The young man comforted the girl as they explained their situation to Kevin. Hank listened.

'And you last saw them when?'

The girl, Aimee, spoke. 'Around midnight. They'd wandered off from the camp. They haven't been back since.'

His eyes darted to Mayor Bob as he left the building.

You son of a bitch. This is what happens when you won't let me do my job.

Kevin spotted Hank and explained, 'Two missing teenagers.'

Joining Kevin at the desk, Hank asked the couple,

'They went missing last night?'

The young man, Nick, answered. 'We thought they'd gone to... Well... You know...' He blushed a little. Hank was unfazed.

'Was this before or after the earthquake?'

'Just before,' Aimee said.

Hank nodded, taking Kevin's notes and giving them a glance over. He tried to reassure Aimee. 'I'll put out a description. If you give all of their details to Deputy Payton here, I'll make sure all Rangers are on the alert. It's most likely they've just wandered off, gotten lost. Happens all the time. Busy season like this, they're usually not lost for long. Try not to worry about it.'

Aimee nodded, somewhat placated. But Nick watched Hank's expression. He saw the look of concern hidden beneath Hank's mask of repose. At that moment, Nick was doubtful that he would see his friend ever again. He held Aimee's hand a little tighter as they turned to leave.

Hank turned away and spoke conspiratorially to Deputy Kevin, 'Can I borrow you for just a second?'

'Sure, boss.'

They moved away from the desk, out of ear shot of Aimee and Nick. Hank spoke in a hushed tone. 'Listen, I'm gonna take Lori up to take a look at those geysers. She reckons there's more to last night's tremor than we saw. Could be a public safety issue.'

'How so?'

Hank had to admit, 'I don't know yet. Could be nothing, could be something unstable, dormant. Look, I don't want to cause a panic, but the Mayor won't let us investigate this properly. Until you get the all clear from me, I need you to have everyone on alert, you understand?' He knew he wasn't giving Deputy Kevin much to work with, but he needed him to trust him. At least until Lori could offer some assurances.

Kevin nodded, 'Sure thing.'

In the corner of his eye, Hank spotted Nick watching him, trying to read his lips. He turned away. 'Tell no one.'

Turning from his Deputy, Hank crossed to Lori's temporary office. Nick led Aimee out of the Ranger Station.

The office was filled with clutter. Paperwork, random cables and wires, bags and cases brimming with equipment. Hank wondered if Lori had raided the University store room before she came. How much was all this stuff worth? Despite the fact that the office had been given to Lori, she seemed reluctant to make a home of it. The drawers and desk were empty, like a Motel she was stopping at for the night. Hank knew Lori had never intended to make his park a permanent base, but from her initial reservations he felt she was starting to enjoy herself here.

A heavy rucksack full of supplies was swung on to Lori's back and she adjusted herself as she saw Hank waiting expectantly.

'You ready?'

Lori smiled and nodded. An expedition with the Sheriff. If nothing else, it was a good chance to get to know him better. He seemed to be a decent guy. For a local.

'You're really taking all this stuff?'

Having forgotten a cable, she snatched it from the floor, wrapped it in her hand and stuffed it in to her shorts pocket. 'Never know when I'm gonna need it.'

'I tried to buy us some time with the Mayor,' Hank explained.

'And?'

Hank shook his head.

'Then I guess we need to get some answers quickly.'

Lori was right. Some hard figures may convince Mayor Bob. If not, perhaps Hank needed to call an impromptu press conference, embarrass the Mayor in to taking action. The possibilities swam around in Hank's mind, but he was pulled from his reverie by a shout from Deputy Kevin.

'Hank? Is that your daughter outside?'

Sophie? Why would Sophie come up to the park today. He stuck his head out of Lori's office door, giving Kevin a puzzled look.

And then it dawned on him.

Kevin said, 'She's picking a fight with some guys.'

His daughter, the activist. The start of hunting season. What better time for a teenager to undermine her father's authority. He rolled his eyes to Lori, excusing himself. Through gritted teeth, he said, 'I'll meet you out front, I've just got to...'

Lori nodded, grinning.

It was their Christmas.

Old school friends spending a weekend together, hunting, drinking, reminiscing. Ed could think of nothing better in the whole world. They were hardly the academic type, but they were good with their hands and determined. Once they had left school, their careers had spread them across the United States.

Ed had spent time working on rigs around Alaska after serving overseas. The cold never bothered him and he had plenty of time to himself, which suited him.

Brad had moved to Colorado and started a successful logging company. Ed had on occasion seen Brad's trucks as far north as Washington. It was reassuring to see that a drop out could make it.

Dennis had stayed local. He worked at a Guns and Ammo Outlet until it closed down and moved to online sales. He went back to college and became a plumber. Ed was always glad that Dennis had stayed at home. It gave them a reason to get back together yearly, visit old haunts, check up on old girlfriends.

Ed and Brad had arrived in town two days previous. They spent a night in a guest house before driving out to Dennis' cabin, stocking up on supplies and heading out. With their arsenal piled high in the back of Dennis' truck, they now loaded supplies from the Ranger Station in amongst them. But they had found themselves the target of protesters. Unabated, Dennis stocked up as Sophie followed closely behind.

'You think it's fair, huh? Big men with their toys hunting an animal. You think you're so tough. Well, how about you try taking it on without all them guns, huh? Not so tough then, are you? You know what you are? You're just a bunch of cowards. Lousy, redneck cowards.'

Ed laughed from beside the truck. He chewed his tobacco as he listened to the tirade, then decided to be just as provocative. 'Now, don't be getting your panties in a twist there, girlie.'

'Girlie?' As intended, this just incensed Sophie further, who marched across to Ed and squared up to him. 'Who are you calling girlie?'

'Oh, I am sorry,' Ed sneered derisively, 'How is it you dykes like to be addressed these days?'

She couldn't help herself. Fist clenched, Sophie swung hard, but her arm was caught and in a heartbeat she was dragged away from Ed, who laughed.

Hank pointed an accusatory finger in his daughter's face. 'Didn't I tell you to stay at home?'

'Did you hear what he just called me?'

'You shouldn't be here.'

'Why?' Sophie folded her arms defensively, 'Ashamed to see your little girl stood alongside the protestors?'

Now it was Hank's turn to go on the defensive. How was she so good at turning these scenarios around? Just like her mother. 'That's not the case, and you know it.' Hank would never arrest his daughter. He was more likely to start swinging punches at those who belittled her protest. Whether he liked what she was doing or not, she was still his little girl and he wouldn't stand for anyone insulting her. He needed her to go home, if not for herself but to ensure he didn't do anything he'd regret.

Then he thought of the earthquake. There was something bigger than the protest. She was safer at home.

'Besides, it's not safe here today.'

'For who? Me or the bears?'

'Stop it,' Hank didn't have time to argue with her today. He took a breath. 'Look, stay right here. Don't cause any more trouble. I'm just going up to the geysers, as soon as I get back I'll take you home. Deal?'

Sophie just stared at him. Hank nodded and turned to walk away.

'Why do you let them do it, Dad?'

He stopped, turning back towards her. He pleaded with her, 'It's not up to me, baby. You know that.' It was a conversation they had every Hunting Season since she was old enough to reason. When she was little, she would cry. It broke his heart, but there was nothing he could do.

'But you're the Park Ranger. You're supposed to look after everything, not let people destroy it.'

'It's population control.' It was cold, but there was nothing else he could say. It wasn't that he disagreed with his daughter – but he did have a job to do.

Sophie grunted, 'Avon says the only population control we need is Mother Nature herself.' Immediately, she felt her cheeks flush. She knew she shouldn't have mentioned Avon to her father.

Hank's demeanour changed. His back straightened, his face stiffened. 'Avonaco is a crazy old man. I thought I'd told you not to go up there?'

Avonaco, a park resident. Avon lived in a log cabin in the hills overlooking the Park. His Native American heritage trail was a hit with the tourists, but Hank didn't like the idea of Sophie and her friends listening to what Hank often described as *hippy sixties bullshit.*

Chastised, Sophie tried to change tact, 'I'm seventeen, Dad. I'm old enough to make my own decisions.' Smooth. Way to sound like the adult.

'Hanging around with a guy who approaches bears is not a good decision. He's dangerous. That kind of shit would get you killed.' Hank knew his daughter understood, but her stubbornness caused him concern. Not least of which because he knew where she got it from. 'I don't want you going to Avonaco's, understood?'

Sophie nodded, silent.

Hank leaned in, kissing his daughter on the forehead. 'I've got to go back to work. Stay with Deputy Kevin. And try not to punch any more guys with guns, okay? There's a limit to how far I'll go to defend you, you know. Loaded weapons is one of those limits.' He gave his daughter a wink. She backed away as Hank started towards the Jeep. Lori stood waiting, her bags loaded in to the back.

'You mean you wouldn't do anything for me?' Sophie grinned, teasing.

Hank held his hands up, 'You're seventeen remember? Old enough to make your own decisions?' Pulling his tongue at Sophie, Hank then turned to the Jeep and climbed in beside Lori. Sophie watched as the Jeep roared to life and left a trail of dust in its wake as it cut a trail up the dirt path towards the hills. She felt two people at her shoulder – her friends, Tyler and Carly.

'You told him we went to see Avon?' Carly pouted.

Sophie shrugged, defensively, 'I tell my Dad everything. What's wrong with that?'

Tyler grunted, 'If my Mom finds out I'll be grounded for life.'

'Relax,' Sophie smiled, 'My Dad's cool.' She turned back to the Ranger Station, to the Hunters stood loading supplies, checking ammo and sipping beer. Her resolve returned, 'Now is this a protest or what? Where are those placards?'

CHAPTER 4

Nick and Aimee slowly staggered back to their tent as the teen revellers around them conducted some minor repairs to their tents. The earthquake had snapped a few tentpoles, disrupted a few campfires and upset a few trees. Those with their tents near the edges of the clearing had decided to uproot, moving their tents closer to the centre and out of the path of any further uprooting. Not that the earthquake had dampened the mood – in fact, the party was ready to begin all over again. Music was being cranked back up, the cleared pile of bottles and cans was starting to rebuild itself.

Nick and Aimee were not in the mood to join the revelry. They were still pondering their journey to the Ranger Station. And it appeared their friends had not returned in their absence. Aimee was deep in thought.

'Did you buy all that back there?' Nick asked.

Aimee was distracted, 'What?'

'That crap about people going missing all the time. You saw the look on that Sheriff's face. He's scared.' He realised that this was probably not the most calming thing he could say. Aimee was clearly holding back some tears.

Nick thought better of continuing his train of thought and slowly moved to his tent.

After a few minutes, Aimee was more composed. 'You think this is all linked to the earthquake?'

'Could be.'

Aimee tried to downplay matters as she thought them through. 'But if things were really that dangerous, why would they keep the park open?'

It was a question Nick had pondered all the way back to camp. In truth, there was no answer. 'Big business, I guess,' Nick speculated. Aimee didn't respond. He sat himself down beside the extinguished campfire. On the grass opposite him, Lisa's discarded sweater lay where she had sat. Next to it, the discarded beer bottle of Nick's friend Jake.

He thought back to last night. What time had they left? He had been too drunk to notice. He remembered retreating to his own tent with Aimee. Nick shared the tent with Jake, so if he wasn't there…

Scanning the camp, Lisa's tent had collapsed in the earthquake. It still lay in a heap on the floor amongst the most densely populated plots of land. Behind it, tall grass led through the trees.

Lisa wouldn't want to be heard with Jake, he surmised. They must have snuck out behind her tent. He craned his neck from his seat. Thinking out loud, he asked Aimee, 'Which way did you think they went?'

Aimee stirred, following Nick's line of sight. 'Wait, you're not seriously thinking of going after them?' Nick stood, moving toward Lisa's flattened tent. Behind it, the long grass was broken.

Someone had passed through.

'They could have been in a landslide,' Aimee reasoned, 'or fallen down something.'

Nick moved at a pace now. 'You don't want to help?'

Trailing behind, Aimee appeared reluctant. 'Of course I do. They were my friends too. I just don't think it's such a good idea to wander off right now.'

Nick brushed off her concerns as he reached the tall grass. 'Just a quick look and we'll come right back.' Aimee found she was still following behind, against her better judgement. She kept glancing back, hoping to catch someone's eye – someone who might prevent them leaving, who would at least bear witness to their departure. When she turned back, Nick was gone.

'Nick!' She quickened her pace to try and catch him. The foliage grew dense and she had to swipe branches aside as she weaved through the forest. 'I can't believe I'm following you.'

'Then wait at the campsite.' Nick's voice came from her left. She turned to follow his voice. He was close by, but the crunch and pop of twigs and roots indicated that Nick was moving at a pace.

Behind her, the campsite was now completely obscured. The background chatter was muted by the trees.

Ahead, Nick was drawing further and further away. Aimee started to panic. She'd made a few turns since leaving the camp, she wasn't sure she could find her way back without him.

She ran to catch up, but stumbled. Her foot caught a root. Instinctively, Aimee reached out to stop her fall, her hands finding the trunk of a large tree. Her eyes were drawn to the base of the tree trunk.

There was blood.

'Nick!'

She heard him stop, then hurry towards her. Aimee turned away, she couldn't look. The thought of this being the blood of her friend made her queasy.

Nick emerged from the bushes, drawn towards the dark stain underneath the tree. He crouched down to examine it. Slowly, he reached out his hand. Aimee could see that it shook.

'Don't touch it!'

'Why not?'

'It's evidence!'

Nick's finger prodded the bloodstain. It was sticky, thick and congealed. He rubbed it between his finger and thumb and brought it to his nose. It smelt of iron. 'Well?' Aimee asked, expectantly.

'Well, it isn't tomato juice.'

'Is it human?'

'What do you want me to do?' Nick scoffed, 'Taste it?'

Aimee hesitated, 'Would that work?'

'Are you serious?'

Before Aimee could respond, there was a murmur from the clearing ahead. It grew louder. A rumbling. A deep roar. Nick stood back, taking Aimee's hand. He was poised, ready to run. 'What the hell was that?'

There was another sound that accompanied the roar – low, barely audible. It sounded like conversation.

Aimee looked to Nick, a glimmer of hope running through each of them. Perhaps their friends were still alive, after all…

Jake started towards the sound, shouting, 'Jake? Jake!' Aimee had broken free from Nick's grip and cautiously followed a few paces behind. The conversation was louder, drawing closer and closer. The occasional roar still accompanied them.

Maybe this was a trap. Maybe whatever caught Lisa would catch them too.

Aimee wanted to turn back, to run away from the noise. But she wouldn't leave Nick. Adrenaline forced her to press on. Jake broke in to a sprint as he reached the edge of the forest, bursting through trees into the path of the roaring monster…

…the RV screeched to a halt, inches from Nick's face. He held up his hands as Aimee let out a scream of surprise. The roar had been the engine of the vehicle, fighting its way down a dirt track road. The conversation was from the open window as Saul and Rita argued.

Their dispute had been cut short as Saul had slammed the breaks on, narrowly avoiding Nick.

'Are you crazy, darting out like that? I could have killed you!' shouted Saul from the window. Nick was too stunned to reply. He came to his senses when Aimee grabbed his arm, pulling him from the path of the vehicle.

Aimee apologised to Saul, who pulled the RV up alongside the young couple. 'You need to take more care,' Saul waved a finger at Nick, 'This park, it's full of tourists today. Lucky I'm a careful driver. Some of those maniacs back there, the ones with the guns, they'd be wiping you off their windscreen.' Nick didn't respond. Instead, he bent over and caught his breath. He looked like he might be sick. Aimee stroked his back, concerned.

'Are you all right, honey?' Rita's brow furrowed as she watched them. She could see that Aimee's hands were shaking, Nick's knees were weak, they looked tired.

Aimee replied, 'We were just looking for some friends. Thought they might have come out this way. It's been a rough morning.' Aimee was holding back the tears. Her friends had been missing for fifteen hours and it grew more and more likely that something had happened to them. She tried to push it from her mind, but she found herself dreading the phone call to Lisa's parents – What would she say? What could she have done? She had to keep searching. The Wardens may be stretched thin, but Aimee wouldn't stop.

'Saul, pull up here. These kids look like they could use a tea.' Rita disappeared into the bowels of the RV. Seconds later, the door flung open. Aimee could see a clear kitchen table, which Rita now busied herself to ready for guests.

Aimee hesitated, 'That's sweet, thanks, but we've really...'

Rita cut her off, shouting from the kitchen, 'I'll hear no more about it. You come sit down. You've had quite the scare.'

Aimee looked to Nick for support. He was still in shock. Her eyes flicked up to Saul, still sat at the steering wheel watching through the open window. Saul shrugged, 'You can't argue with her. I should know.' He gave her a reassuring wink, Aimee smiled back politely. Nick nodded to her and they stepped in to the RV.

The tea brewed.

There was no conversation between Hank and Lori as they sped through the park. Lori continued to study her print outs, occasionally looking up to gauge her location from a bump in the road or a pothole. Hank was thinking of his daughter – her defiant visits to the old Native American mystic. What ideas would he fill her head with? Hank didn't have much time for faith or spiritualism. His daughter was so outspoken, he was surprised to see such a side from her.

Maybe he should go speak to Avonaco himself, set the record straight.

They had never been friends. Avonaco saw Hank as the invader, destroying the natural habitat, making tourist attractions and corporate sponsorships out of something pure, something that should be enjoyed by all. But Hank loved the park. He didn't always agree with the calls made, but they came from a higher power than he.

They passed a sign directing tourists to the geysers. Hank took the turn. In the distance, the steam could be seen rising from the site. To his right, hills dominated the landscape. Amongst them, Avonaco's cabin. He could be watching Hank right now.

His grip on the wheel stiffened.

'Slow down. We're almost there.' Lori snapped him from his reverie.

They came to a halt before the park's largest geyser – a natural spring of volcanic water that erupted frequently. It was the star attraction of the park. Today, the Rangers had closed the geyser off to visitors for safety reasons. It made the rocky flat expanse of the geysers quite uncharacteristically tranquil.

Lori quickly unloaded her equipment from the back of the Jeep – a backpack, her laptop and measuring equipment. Hank watched, fidgeting. Lori carried it alone towards the geyser.

Hank stopped her from getting any closer, 'That's far enough.'

Lori nodded, crouching down and placing the equipment on the floor around her. She opened her laptop and booted up the software. Hank stood at her shoulder, looking to the hills. She tried to ignore him, but his twitching made her nervous.

'Something wrong?'

'No, no...' Hank started, then restrained himself. He let out an exasperated sigh.

Lori shrugged and continued with her work. Hank started to pace behind her. 'It's just...'

Lori finished his sentence. 'Sophie?'

Hank began to open up. He crouched down beside her, noticeably relieved to be offered the chance to unburden himself. 'She shouldn't be out here. She should be back home, at the Mall or at her friends' house.'

'Seriously?' Lori scoffed.

'What?'

She laughed, 'You have a lot to learn about teenage girls.'

Hank stood and started pacing again. 'It's not just that. It's the people she's hanging out with.'

'Seemed a decent crowd to me. Just kids. They've found their voice and started a cause. We all did that.'

Hank practically spat his next word out. 'Avon.'

It took Lori a moment. 'Avonaco? The guy on the hill?'

He nodded. 'The Native American, yeah.'

His derision seemed out of place to Lori. She wondered if there was something more to his dislike of Avonaco. Against her better judgement, she added, 'She could pick worse role models.'

This set Hank off. 'Come on, Lori. He hangs around with hobos and hippies, fills their head with garbage. The 'All Mother' and the 'Great Bear'. It might work on the tourists, but I expect my daughter to know better.'

There was a long pause. Lori looked up at Hank, who seemed somewhat embarrassed by his outburst. He tried to hide it, 'What?'

'People find inspiration from many different places, Sheriff. Whether they're spiritual journeys or just valuable life lessons, you can't dismiss it.' She thought back to their exit from the Ranger Station, to Sophie's defiance in the face of the Hunters. She reminded Lori of Hank. 'Your daughter stood up to those hunters today and fought for something she believed in. That's a trait to be admired, not chastised. Give her a break, huh?'

Hank sighed and settled down beside Lori.

'Maybe you're right.' Perhaps he was spending too much time at the park. Perhaps he needed to spend more time at home, talk to his family, understand them. Hank sat in silent contemplation.

Data continued to stream across Lori's laptop.

Hank watched. 'So what you find?'

Lori sighed. 'So far, nothing.'

'Is that good?'

Lori shrugged, 'Well, there should be some kind of residual disturbance following a 'quake of that magnitude. Like a ripple in a glass of water. You can't feel it, but the equipment should pick it up. I can't find it.'

'So it's bad.'

'It's too early to tell,' Lori explained. But she still couldn't account for the lack of residuals. 'There was that second spike, but I'm not showing any side effects.' She was confused. How could something so big not show up on any readings?

Hank offered his thoughts, 'Maybe the equipment malfunctioned, recorded the same tremor twice.'

It was a line of thought that had occurred to Lori. But the spikes were so different. She shook her head. 'They were two distinct tremors.' She readjusted the settings on screen, focused her search in the hope of some small means of explanation.

What she found surprised her.

'Hold on…' Lori was transfixed by her readings. Hank leaned in close, a vain effort to understand Lori's device. 'I've got something.' She pointed to the screen.

'Good?' Hank asked.

'Confusing, actually.' Lori pointed to a few small ripples that appeared on her graph. 'These spikes are pretty faint, but our proximity to the geyser is amplifying the signal.'

This did not help Hank. 'Is it not what you expected?'

'Well, they tally with the second tremor, but these are too regular to be aftershock. There's a rhythm. Take a look.'

Hank focused on the graph as it recorded the tremors emitting from underneath them. Sure enough, the small spikes in activity had a rhythm. Hank only had one comparator. 'Just looks like a heart monitor to me.'

Lori smiles, Hank was right. 'A heartbeat or steady breathing...'

They considered the possibilities for a moment. What could be down there? How big could it be? Had it caused the tremor? Or was it woken by it?

Hank laughed. 'Something's alive down there?'

Lori shrugged it off. 'Can't be. Not at that size. Not that deep. But I should probably record more data. If I can send my findings to the University, I can get them to take a look.'

Hank nodded, gave Lori a reassuring pat on the back and moved towards the Jeep. He glanced towards the sky and caught sight of a figure watching them from the hills. Avonaco, stood on the outcrop near his cabin. *The old bastard must think he knows exactly what's happening.*

Hank gritted his teeth.

He turned back to Lori, who was now completely engrossed in her work. 'Will you be long?'

Without turning to him, she joked, 'You got somewhere else to be, Sheriff?'

'It's Hank. Call me Hank.' Lori had been around long enough now, she was beginning to feel like part of the team. 'I was just gonna take a drive up to the cabin. Have a talk with our Native friend.'

'Sure. I'll be fine here.'

Hank backed away towards the Jeep. He kept one eye on Avonaco. 'I'll swing by for you in a while. Don't wander too far.'

'I'll be right here.'

Hank swung the door of the Jeep open, climbed in and fired up the engine. He heard his name called over the sound of the Jeep. It was Lori. He wound his window down and leaned out. She smiled at him.

'Go easy on him, huh?'

Hank grunted.

Nick sat with a warm mug of tea in hand, his shock from his near accident now gone. Opposite him, Aimee sat smiling at him. She was enjoying the temporary distraction from finding their friends.

Sat beside him, Rita was enjoying the company. Her husband Saul hung back by the kitchen unit, chiming in as and when his wife would allow.

'So where are you kids from?'

Aimee replied between sips of tea. 'We're studying at Oregon, but I'm originally from Pasadena.'

Rita smiled, 'A beautiful part of the country. We're from out East, been travelling across the country for a couple months now.' Saul was quietly rolling his eyes, having heard his tale being told to many a traveller during their journey. Rita did enjoy telling her story.

'Really?' Aimee enthused, 'That sounds fun.'

Saul scoffed, 'Try living with a chemical toilet for two months. It changes your definition of fun.'

Rita dismissed her husband with a wave of her hand. 'Oh, he's just grumpy because he's been driving eight hours straight. He loves it, really.' She threw him a playful wink and he gave her a wry smile.

Aimee laughed.

'You said you were looking for your friends?' Saul asked.

Nick responded, 'Yes, we reported them missing...'

'I'm sure they'll turn up,' Aimee interrupted. 'We were just a little worried.' She didn't want to alarm the couple. After all, they had nothing to go on at this stage.

Saul continued. 'Must have been worried to run out in front of an RV like that.'

Nick apologised.

Saul's demeanour softened. 'Ah, don't worry about it. With Rita here, I'd have never heard the end of it if I'd hit you! Should have heard her the time I ran over the dog.'

'He says it like it was nothing,' Rita barked, playfully. 'The dog was in a cast for weeks!'

'It just ran out in front of the driveway.'

Rita pointed an accusatory finger at Saul as Aimee giggled. 'He hit it on purpose! He never liked that dog.'

Saul threw an aside to Nick, 'I've always been more of a cat person.'

With Hank gone, tempers had begun to flare once again at the Ranger Station. The young protesters had gotten louder, the amassed hunters became more aggressive and Deputy Kevin's head grew heavier. He leaned against the porch, rubbing his temples and closing his eyes. Below him, a line of placards had been erected. The protesters had now decided to block entry to the Station – effectively preventing the hunters from registering.

The Rangers tried to calm the situation, but tempers were beginning to flare. Hank's daughter Sophie was not helping matters. She now held a megaphone in her hand, mid speech.

'…A dwindling population, policed by men who think they're entitled to kill. Well, the State may have granted you that licence, but their corruption doesn't give you the moral right to kill defenceless animals…'

Deputy Kevin surveyed the crowd. A group of three hunters – Brad, Dennis and Ed – were now ready to roll, their truck fully loaded with supplies. Sophie had gotten in to an altercation with them earlier this morning. Hank had intervened. Deputy Kevin hoped he wouldn't have to step in on behalf of Sophie's father.

'…You have a choice. You can enjoy this park as Mother Nature intended, or you can destroy. But we will not stand by and watch you destroy any longer…'

They climbed in to the truck and Brad revved the engine. But by the time his key had reached the ignition, the protesters had already descended upon them, surrounding the truck. Deputy Kevin groaned.

Brad put his foot down, the engine roared and the protesters flinched.

Not Sophie.

Sophie positioned herself in front of the truck, beckoning to her friends to join her. They did so, reluctantly.

Deputy Kevin found himself stepping down from the porch.

Carly whispered to Sophie, 'Uh, is this such a good idea?'

Tyler nodded, 'They've got pretty big guns, Soph.'

Sophie sneered, 'What are they gonna do? Kill us? Run us over?' She raised the megaphone, staring Brad in the eye. 'Come on, you cowards!'

He edged the car forward. The jerk of the bumper made Carly and Tyler flinch. Sophie was unmoved. The bumper edged closer, closer.

'The big men are scared to run over a girl? Thought you were supposed to be hunters! You don't look so tough to me!'

Brad gritted his teeth. Ed grew nervous. He stuck his head out of the window and shouted to Sophie, 'Hey girl, you'd best step aside. Don't make me move you, now.' He was almost pleading.

'Oh, yeah?'

The protestors cheered Sophie's resolve. Spurned on, she began to kick at the bumper. The engine roared louder. She kicked at the radiator and the headlights. She didn't stop until the radiator was dented. Brad tried to shout, but was drowned out by the rowdy protestors.

The headlamp gave way, the glass cracking. The cheers grew louder.

Seconds later, there was an arm on Sophie's shoulder. Deputy Kevin dragged her from the chaos, rounding up Tyler and Carly as he herded them towards the Ranger Station.

Behind her, Brad took his cue to leave. With his path clear, he put his foot down. The truck sped off in to the forest. Sophie watched it go, then the door to the Ranger Station slammed shut. Deputy Kevin had dragged her inside. The commotion outside was barely audible from the confines of the cabin. It was peaceful to Kevin. He took a few seconds to calm himself down.

'You're in trouble.'

'You're gonna tell my Dad?' Sophie was incensed. She paused, then attempted a manipulative teenager tactic. 'I thought you were cooler than that, Kevin.'

Kevin shook his head. 'That doesn't work on me. You've just caused criminal damage to property. If those guys choose to press charges...'

Sophie cut him off. 'They won't. They're just a bunch of assholes.'

'Either way, you three are gonna sit here until Sheriff Walker comes back.'

Tyler was as furious as a teenage stoner could be, 'Are we like, under arrest, or something?'

'No,' Kevin stopped. 'Kind of.' He growled, 'Just sit down.'

Carly crossed her arms defiantly.

'You have to read us our rights.'

Kevin was exasperated. He looked to Sophie, who offered him no help. 'You have the right to sit down and be quiet.'

'That's oppressive, man.'

'I can always call your parents and explain why I'm detaining you.'

There was a long pause. The three of them sat down. Kevin nodded, satisfied, 'That's what I thought.'

'Deputy Payton?'

The crackly voice came from the radio in the corner. The Deputy turned towards the call. Sophie recognised the voice. It was her Dad, Hank. 'Deputy Payton. Are you there, over?'

Kevin kept his eyes on Sophie as he approached the receiver. She wondered if he would tell him right now. Maybe she had gotten a little carried away…

'I'm receiving you, over.'

'Kevin, I'm just going up to the hill. I've left Lori at the geyser. Any sight of those missing kids, over?'

Missing kids? Sophie looked to her friends. *Just what exactly was going on today?*

Kevin caught her glance. He tried to advise Hank of discretion. 'I'm a little indisposed right now, Hank. I've not had any confirmed sightings, but I'll keep you updated. Over.'

'Understood. I'll check in on my way back. Keep an eye on my daughter for me, will you? Over and out.'

Kevin replaced the receiver. He felt Sophie blush in the corner, embarrassed to hear her father talk about her. Kevin turned to her, 'You heard your father. That's my cue to keep you here out of harm's way.'

Sophie tried to change the subject, 'Who are the missing kids?'

'You weren't supposed to hear that.'

'But we did. Come on, Deputy Kev. Spill the beans.'

Kevin tried to walk away, 'No way.'

But Sophie was undeterred. She crossed her arms. 'Well, we can either help you with your investigation, or we can go back out there and rejoin the protest. Which would you prefer?'

Deputy Kevin rolled his eyes and muttered, 'I'm stuck here with the kids from the Mystery Machine.'

Sophie smiled, 'I'll take it as a compliment.'

Ed stood building a fire in the quiet clearing in which they had decided to make camp. To his right, Dennis put the finishing touches on his tent. It was the last to be erected – Brad and Ed's tents had been completed whilst Dennis unloaded the beer. Now Brad sat in the door of his tent, sorting through a loose box of ammo contentedly. He picked up a large bullet and admired it for a moment, 'Plan on giving the new rifle a spin this weekend.'

Ed snorted. He knew how busy the park could get. 'Enjoy it while it lasts. Soon as this campsite fills up, you'll be clamorin' for bear. That's why it pays to get here early.'

Dennis took a step back, admiring his handiwork. His tent was a little crooked, but sturdy. 'You know the best place to hunt?'

'Damn straight,' Ed nodded, 'Been here every season since I was old enough to carry a pistol.' He pointed through the trees to a crevasse at the base of the hills. 'There's a network of caves just a mile up from here. Bears don't seem to like them, for some reason. Seems to me ideal for hibernatin', but they make a good hide for any that be passin' by.'

Brad was still sore from his encounter with Sophie. He snarled, looking to his dented fender. 'Way I see it, we ought take a bear skin back for that little bitch that done dented my truck. See how she likes it.'

Ed waved him off. He had watched how the Sheriff had spoken to her earlier in the morning, how the Deputy had protected the little vandal. 'Eh, that little bitch is just loud 'cos she's the daughter of the Sheriff. Thinks she can act all high and mighty. She ain't nuthin'.'

Brad laughed. 'I'll drink to that.'

Ed took a beer from the cooler and sat back, thinking about his caves nearby. He explored them every summer as a kid. They were quiet, deep and unoccupied. A perfect spot to wait and hunt.

And the cave's residents were thinking the exact same thing.

CHAPTER 5

The incense burned beside a small ornamental totem. Avonaco sat before it, watching the smoke rise, discerning shapes and patterns as the wisps twisted and turned. He took a deep breath, inhaling the incense as he did so.

He looked up at the totem. The carved wooden features stared down at him. Atop, a grizzly bear growled down at him.

The features of the bears face twitched in the light of the burning candles, the fierce stare of the carved face looked more menacing than he had ever seen and he wondered what it meant.

He meditated.

Something was wrong, today. The air felt close, an unbearable heat and a taste came to his tongue.

Ash?

Before he could consider anything further, a Jeep approached. He crossed to the window, opening the blind to observe. It was Sheriff Hank.

Avon stepped outside to greet him. It wasn't often that the Sheriff visited his cabin. And Avon wasn't the type to go socialising with the Rangers. They all kept a respectful distance from each other.

'Hank, how are you?' Avon offered.

Hank gave him a surly nod. 'Avonaco.'

Avon extended his hand, but Hank refused to acknowledge it. Avon changed tact. 'Would you like to come in? I can make some coffee.'

He sensed Hank's hesitation. The Sheriff looked to the open door of the cabin. Avon glanced back, following his gaze. The totem was visible and the incense wafted through the open door. Avon could sense Hank's scepticism.

'I won't keep you. I can see you're busy,' he said, sarcastically.

Avon chose to ignore the sarcasm and continued warmly, 'It's no trouble. Please.'

With a grunt, Hank reluctantly entered Avon's home. Avon offered him a chair and Hank sat, staring icily at the totem. Avon opened the blinds, the light streamed in and he blew the candles out.

He went to the kitchen and returned with a steaming cup of fresh coffee. He offered it to Hank, snapping him from his reverie.

'Uh, thanks.'

Avon sat opposite Hank, noticed him looking quizzically at the totem. He tried to explain, 'The life totem, indicating the order of things. The Great Bear, the All Mother's representative on Earth, stationed at the very pinnacle of all...'

Hank cut him off, rudely. 'Spare me the history lesson.'

Avon was taken aback. 'I was merely satisfying your curiosity.'

'This kind of spiritual crap might fly with the tourists and...' he hesitated. Avon realised what this was about. He was angry that Sophie had brought her friends up here. Hank collected his thoughts. 'It might fly with the kids, but I'm the Ranger. I'm here to look out for this park, not be mesmerised by some Native American rituals.'

'We all have our part to play,' Avon said, calmly.

'Some of us aren't here to play,' he shouted, tapping the shield on his uniform. He instantly regretted it. He calmed himself, ashamed of his outburst.

'Hank, I always find your choice of words... refreshing. You're honest, I can't fault that.' Avon looked concerned, 'But today you seem troubled. I trust this isn't a social call.'

Hank was blunt. 'Has my daughter and her friends been coming up here?'

Avon was surprised that Sophie had not mentioned it to her father. 'They visit occasionally, yes. Their class is studying Native American history. I've been giving them some information for their assignment.'

'And filling their head with all this garbage?' He pointed to the totem.

Avon was hurt. 'I'm hardly corrupting your child, Hank. I'm just telling a few stories, same as the tourists get. What do you take me for?'

'I take you to be some crazy old man who lives on a hill, alone in the middle of a National Park, who talks to bears.' Hank leaned in. He was furious. 'Or have I read that wrong?'

There was no reasoning with Hank when he was in this sort of mood. Avon suspected there was more to this. The earthquake, perhaps? It was a busy season for the Rangers. Hank looked like he was lacking some sleep. Avon chose to relent, 'That about sums it up, I guess. But I'm not exactly presenting my stories as fact, Hank. They're fables, passed down by generations. They're at an impressionable age, I get that. But is there anything wrong with them learning some ancient cultures and customs?'

Hank calmed himself down. 'I'm sorry, Avon. She's a loose cannon. I've just caught her protesting at the Station, picking fights with guys with guns. It's scary.'

Avon sympathised. 'I know how it is, Hank. No need to apologise. But where I'm concerned, it's just a few folk tales from my family. Kids like that, Native American mysticism is probably just a phase. They've found something that flies in the face of conventional thinking and they've embraced it. I'd be lying if I said I hadn't enjoyed the company. They listen quietly, unlike the tourists!'

Both men shared a laugh.

Hank hesitated.

'You know I worry about her,' he said, sipping from his coffee.

'So you should. You're her father. I would have a problem if you didn't,' Avon laughed.

'And it's dangerous up here,' Hank continued, 'Avon, you have bears wandering back and forth like they're pets.'

'I have one bear,' Avon corrected, 'And he's a friend. A spirit guide.'

'You see?'

'Honestly, it's safer up here than it is amongst your hunters, or those missing kids.'

Hank shot him a look. 'How'd you hear about that?'

Avon closed his eyes, 'On the wind, my friend.' Hank stared at him. Avon gave a wry smile. 'Deputy Kevin gave me a radio,' he said, deadpan. 'I pick up on some of your chatter now and again.'

Hank considered his coffee, hands wrapped around it warmly. 'Lori thinks it may be linked to last night's earthquake.'

'The seismology student?'

Hank nodded, 'She's out at the geyser right now. Thinks there might have been some residual activity.'

It explained the feeling Avon had during his meditation. He pondered aloud, 'The All Mother is angry. The hunters are gathering.'

Hank said nothing.

Avon caught the look that Hank gave him. 'You can roll your eyes, Hank, but there's something in the air. I can taste... fire. People shouldn't be here, Hank.'

Hank felt the same way, but there was no convincing some people.

The amassed crowd at the Ranger Station now gathered at the porch. A few local reporters held microphones up in front of Mayor Brady, who addressed the people.

He did this every year, officially opening the

Hunting Season. It was good publicity for his office. And keeping the local rednecks and hillbillies happy was how he won a re-election.

He raised his hands, mid speech.

'So without further delay, it gives me great pleasure to announce that this year's Bear Season is officially...'

He stopped. There was a long rumbling under his feet.

'What the hell is that?' he muttered, forgetting his proximity to the microphone. The reporters murmured. Another earthquake? People looked ready to panic. He tried to reassure them, 'If we can all remain calm, I'm sure there's no cause for alarm.'

But the rumbling grew louder.

The Mayor realised this was not an earthquake.

It was a stampede.

The trees rustled. Suddenly, hundreds of small animals came racing through. squirrels, chipmunks, raccoons, skunks, all came thundering down on the Ranger Station. The crowd was startled. A few of them screamed, but the animals were unperturbed.

It was like they were fleeing in blind panic.

Leaving the park.

The crowd huddled together, covering themselves, flinching, some broke away running for cover.

The Mayor watched dumbfounded as a Skunk jumped in to his arms.

Reporters ran for their vans. The cameramen filmed on, bemused.

Inside the Ranger Station sat Sophie, Carly and Tyler – grounded by Sheriff Hank. They watched the animals flee from the window. Deputy Kevin peered out in surprise.

'What in the name of...'

'Something's spooked them,' Sophie observed. 'Look. They're all moving in the one direction. It's like an exodus.'

'Maybe they all saw something,' Tyler speculated.

Outside, squirrels clambered over cars, skunks ran through the legs of the panicked crowd, a flock of birds smashed against the outside broadcast transmitter on top of news vans as they hurriedly tried to dodge it. Hordes of mice scurried for holes in the wall of the Station. A man tripped on a dog, falling flat on his face as a wave of chipmunks ran across his back, in too much of a hurry to go around him.

The Mayor ran to his car. He started the engine, put his foot through the accelerator and tried to speed away.

Suddenly, a bird smashed through his windscreen, flapping its wings furiously. It flew away, unharmed, but the Mayor lost control. The car rolled in to a nearby tree.

One of the many hunters pulled out a rifle, aiming at the dense population of animals. As he swung it, the critters forced him to lose his balance. He fell backwards, shooting in to the air, causing the crowd to duck for cover.

The animals scattered, the damage done.

People raised their heads from their cover. All was still again.

Lori continued to isolate the signal coming from beneath the geyser. She tapped at her keyboard, sat on the valley floor. She muttered to herself, deep in thought.

'If I can just isolate...'

She tapped away furiously. The spike of activity on her screen was converted in to a sound clip.

She enhanced it, then hit play.

Lori struggled to hear it over the sound of the geyser. She turned her volume to maximum and held the laptop speaker up to her ear.

The sound was not what she expected.

Breathing.

The slow, raspy breath of disturbed sleep.

'Oh, shit.'

Lori minimised the sound file, then brought up the second spike recorded last night - the alleged aftershock. A realisation crept across her face.

Reaching for her cell phone, she dialled the Sheriff.

Hank took his final gulp of coffee as his cell phone began to ring. He put the mug down and looked apologetically to Avon.

'Sorry, I gotta...'

'Go ahead,' Avon said.

The Caller ID showed 'LORI'. He answered and said, 'I'm just finishing up here. Shouldn't be more than a few...'

Lori cut him off, sounding panicked, 'Hank, we have a problem here.'

'What's up?'

She spoke fast. 'I've analysed the rhythmic signal I found at the geyser. It's not aftershock. I managed to enhance the sound, run it through a few filters...'

'Tell me,' Hank prompted.

'It's breathing. Hank, something's alive down there. And I think the earthquake has disturbed it.'

Hank was confused. 'Alive? Like what? Like an animal?'

'It's too loud to be one animal. To register like this, there's got to be a lot them.'

He had no idea what she was talking about. He tried to calm her down, 'A lot of what?'

'I can't tell. We need to get this park evacuated.' She was serious.

Hank tried to rationalise this. 'Whatever it is, it's not just appeared. It's got to have been there for some time. How can we be sure it's such a threat?' It was a reasonable question.

'This is all just speculation, Hank, but that aftershock last night; I think it came from Them. Whatever is sleeping down there, I think last night's 'quake woke them up.'

Hank paused, trying to maintain his composure.

'Sit tight. I'm on my way,' he said, gravely.

He put his cell phone back in his pocket and paced towards the door. Avon watched him, surprised.

'I have to go.'

'Something happened?' Avon asked, concerned.

Hank considered, 'You should come too. I need to get everyone out of the park.'

'Another earthquake?'

'Worse.' Hank threw open the door to the cabin. 'Will you come with me?'

Avon shook his head. 'Do what you need to do, Hank. I'm protected.' He turned back to his totem.

Hank didn't have time to argue. He stepped through the door and raced off toward his Jeep. Avon watched the Sheriff depart.

The geyser sprayed a burst of hot volcanic water in to the air beside Lori. She started to pack her equipment away, hurriedly.

Another spray from the geyser. Far more regular than she expected. She felt another disturbance coming and she stopped. Her laptop was still open beside her. The readings on the seismograph were beginning to spike once again.

The earth started to tremor.

The geyser erupted, more sustained, more violently.

Then there was a jerk. The ground shuddered. Lori staggered backward, away from the geyser, struggling to maintain her footing.

As the ground shook, the geyser erupted, the pressure building up from below released.

Lori stopped.

Beneath the volcanic spray, she thought she heard something.

It was faint, coming from deep within the earth.
It was a roar.

CHAPTER 6

The teacups started to dance across the table, excitedly. Aimee reached out and steadied the nearest cup. Another danced towards the edge of the table and Nick caught it just in time.

Saul was impressed with Nick's reflexes.

'Another earthquake?'

The trembling became more violent, the cupboards rattled and banged open. The motor home shook from side to side, its fixtures juddering, cupboards falling open and the contents crashing to the floor. Rita panicked and Saul hurried to her, protecting his wife from the falling cutlery and dishes.

Aimee rushed to the door of the motor home. She opened it and peered out as the forest violently shook. The trees swayed beside them, bushes rattling and the road warped slightly.

There was a *ROAR*.

It was so loud, so close.

Rita covered her ears. A chill ran up Saul's spine.

Ed waved his friends over to his position. He was

crouched next to a great big tree trunk. They started towards him but he signalled for them to stay low. They crouched alongside him, rifles down.

They followed Ed's gaze. He had a deer in his sights.

It stood alone, eating the long grass.

Dennis nodded to his friends – he wanted this one. They gave him the signal and he edged forward, lifting his rifle, sighting the deer dead centre. He took a deep, calming breath and put his finger to the trigger.

The ground shook.

The deer was lost in his sight, he couldn't take the shot. He swore under his breath as he tried to steady himself, but the 'quake was persistent. He lost his footing, falling back on to his rear – much to the amusement of his friends.

The deer darted away in to the dense forest.

'Fuck,' Dennis complained, 'I could have had him.'

He climbed to his feet, waving his arms angrily as his friends stepped forward.

'He was right there!'

Out of nowhere, a huge shape pounced on Dennis. He swung around, rifle in hand, landing on his back, desperately fending off his attacker with the rifle. His friends ran to him, shouting and firing wildly.

It was a bear.

It looked like a bear. It was bear shaped.

But it was twice the size of any grizzly Ed had ever encountered at the park. And its hide looked tough. Not your typical fur.

Not that it mattered. Dennis was about to be eaten.

That's when the loud *ROAR* erupted from deep in the forest. Whatever this was, there was more of them.

Dennis struggled, his rifle stretched across its face, fending of the gnashing teeth of his attacker. He stared in to its eyes.

They burnt with fire. Blood red. He had never seen eyes so terrifying.

Saliva dripped on to Dennis' chest as he fought for his life. Ed and Brad fired their rifles in to the dark hide of the giant bear, but the bullets had no effect on its tough fur. It was like armour. As thick as a Rhino hide. And underneath it, there was a glimmer of deep orange...

They were helpless. They couldn't fend it off. Their bullets had no effect. They tried to club it with their rifle butts, but it wouldn't budge. And all the while, it gnashed its teeth in Dennis' face while his friends struggled on futilely.

Aiming for its face, Dennis brought his rifle butt around and smacked it on the snout as hard as he could. It was like punching a brick wall.

They suddenly heard a scream.

A young girl had stepped through the trees and come upon their fight – wandering out from the students' camp. She stood petrified as the hunters were momentarily distracted.

The bear swung around, its hungry eyes locked on the young girl.

Dennis used the momentary reprieve to scramble free from underneath the bear. Ed helped drag him to safety.

The bear jumped up and darted towards the girl. She was frozen to the spot.

Brad shouted to her, *'RUN!'* and she turned and darted back through the trees.

Another roar. This one was close.

Brad turned. Two more bears – as large and as hideous as the first - stood on a rise, looking down at the hunters. Dennis scrambled to his feet and they darted in the opposite direction, leaping fallen logs and branches as the bears began their pursuit.

The girl ran. She couldn't look round, she dare not see the bear bounding behind her. She was close to the camp, she could outrun it. Just a few more feet and she would be safe.

She had to warn them all.

Don't go in to the woods. If they did, they would be sure of a big surprise.

The branches of the trees caught her in the face, whipping her as she sprinted to safety. Her face was cut, her arms beaten and bruised from knocking the large roots out of her path.

She could hear the party. She was home free. The bear must have given up the chase. No matter. She had to press on. Don't slow down.

Bursting through the trees, she tripped over a tent pole and fell in to the camp, rolling to a halt right in the centre.

Nobody noticed. The drunken revelry continued regardless.

'BEAR!' she screamed.

There was no reaction. The music continued to play. The dancing and the drinking were uninterrupted.

She stood, catching her breath.

Did that just happen? Was she dreaming?

A few moments passed. The more she thought about the bear, the more she doubted herself. It was some great rock monster, mauling some redneck guy.

Did I drop some acid, or something?

She took another few breaths, her heart rate relaxed and she waved the whole experience off as a particularly lucid dream. She turned back towards the forest path.

The bear stood there, looming over her. Silent.

Its giant claws lunged for her, grabbing her by the shoulders and tearing both arms from her sockets with ease. She spun around, the blood spurting from her open wounds like a lawn sprinkler.

Now her fellow campers saw her. They jumped up, terrified and started to run for their lives.

It was too late for her.

The bear bit down on her head.

The tremor began to subside. Lori watched it fade on her seismograph. She surveyed the ground around her. There were fresh cracks present around the geyser. The ground had literally opened up. Along the path, a few trees were leaning, uprooted.

There was a hiss. The steaming and bubbling of the geyser. Water started to froth from the fresh cracks, spreading out. She stepped back.

Hank will be here any minute. We need to get back.

There was a noise behind her.

Not the hiss of the geyser or a rumbling that she may expect. This was something living, breathing beside her.

It gave a snort.

CHAPTER 7

Lori tried to control her breathing, her chest tight, her heart pounding. She turned her head ever so slightly, her eyes strained in the corner – desperate to see what was behind her without any sudden body movements.

Another grunt.

There was definitely something there. The crunch of rocks under a massive body. Slowly she turned her head.

The great, hulking bear stood up on its hind legs, its attention drawn to her. Saliva dripped from its huge jaws, its eyes wide with hunger. And a smell. The smell of sulphur.

Lori couldn't help but gasp. As she did, the bear dropped on to all four legs and started towards her.

It was still at the other side of the valley. But she knew that once it gathered a pace, it could easily outrun her.

Looking down, she found her hands fumbling with her equipment – packing it away in to her backpack.

Fuck the equipment. Go!

And then her legs took over. She ran. Her legs quivered, her muscles weak with fear but she couldn't falter. Her eyes darted around, desperate for shelter, but on the expansive floor of the valley, there was none to give.

A snort of hunger.

All she could do was run towards the dirt road.

A roar, this time ahead of her.

This wasn't a bear. Hurtling down the mountain pass was Hank's Jeep. Did she have enough time to reach it? She hazarded a glance behind her.

The bear was bounding now, fury building in its eyes – and, she thought, a hint of a red glow...

She willed herself on, pushing harder, sprinting further.

Only one obstacle lay between her and the Jeep now. A medium sized geyser, steam rising from the crack in the earth. Boiling hot water and steam burst forth from it, but Lori had a plan.

It was all about timing.

Hank could see what Lori planned. The Jeep screeched to a halt and Hank threw open the passenger door.

The bear gained ground. It was so close now.

She could hear it, the sound of paws thumping against the dirt, growing louder and louder behind her. The body heat -

- *Jesus, this thing must be overheating* -

- She could feel the warmth emanating from it as it got nearer and nearer. Like her back was turned to a great bonfire.

The steam obscured her vision as she stepped in to the vicinity of the erupting geyser. The ground rumbled – from an impending eruption or the heavy footfall of the bear, it didn't matter to her. She just knew she had to keep running.

Lori nearly tripped, her foot catching in the broken ground. She lifted her knees higher, her movements measured – but this only slowed her down.

All the while, the bear followed relentless. His pace unfaltering.

Directly ahead, the bubbling of the geyser became more intense, ready to erupt. Lori braced herself, she covered her face and eyes as she raced in to the impending eruption.

She thought she could hear Hank shouting just beyond the hiss of the geyser.

No turning back now.

The breathing almost touched her neck.

Lori jumped.

She cut through the fresh, boiling steam, her skin scalded by the heat. But she kept running.

The rumbling grew louder.

The Bear was so close now.

It leaped through the geyser, a few feet behind her, near enough to taste her...

The geyser erupted, a violent boiling jet of water hit the bear square in the face, knocking the Bear backwards off its feet, screeching to a halt. Its hide boiled as it writhed.

Lori dared not turn to look. She kept running.

Hank waved her onward triumphantly.

She jumped in beside him.

'That was close,' Hank sighed with relief.

'Hold on.' She stopped Hank from reaching for the gas. Instead, she grabbed a pair of binoculars from the dashboard and gazed at the bear. 'Look at the size of that thing.' The hide was so thick that it almost seemed to be plated. She recalled the body heat it gave off, the red of its eyes.

Hank shook his head, 'I've never seen anything like it.'

'How many do you think are out there?'

This time Hank put his foot down on the accelerator. The engine of the Jeep roared. 'Let's not wait to find out.'

They screeched back up the path. 'Where are we going?'

Hank's gaze was intense.

'My daughter's at the Station.'

Brad caught himself from tripping on a tree root. His rifle slid from his shoulder. A hand clasped him by the arm. He gazed in to the panic stricken face of Ed. 'Come on!' He dragged Brad, his hands shook as he clutched the rifle.

'Where's Dennis?'

Their friend had fallen behind. He gasped for breath. Brad reached out to him. 'Keep moving.'

'I can't go on.'

'Stop and you're dead.' He dragged him and

together they fumbled their way through the heavy undergrowth.

Brad was sure it had followed them, but the trees behind them were undisturbed. Still, they carried on.

A snort from the trees to their right.

Another bear, waiting, watching.

Ed readied his gun, 'They're toying with us, man!'

There was no time. They didn't stand a chance, weapons or not. Brad screamed at his friend to keep moving.

Up ahead, there was light. A way out of the thick foliage.

At least then they could see what they were contending with.

They pressed on.

Saul stood at the kitchen window of his motor home, staring out in to the forest. At the table, Rita sat shaking. Aimee helped her take a sip of tea to steady her nerves. Nick paced nervously.

Turning to the young man, Saul shrugged, 'Maybe we should go out there.'

Rita barked, 'Go out there? Are you out of your mind, Saul? There could be animals!'

Saul rolled his eyes. 'It was an earthquake, Rita.'

Aimee looked to Nick for reassurance. 'Sounded like a roar.' Nick said nothing, but gave a quick nod. He could sense that the tremor was more than just an earthquake.

'Nothing roars like that,' Saul continued, 'I should

know.'

Nick looked puzzled. 'Were you in the Army?'

'No, my Uncle Gene owned a Zoo.'

Nick and Aimee shared a smile. Saul gave them both a knowing wink. The group let out a sigh and paused. 'So what do we do now?' Aimee asked.

Nick shrugged silently.

There was a sudden rush of activity outside.

BANG! BANG!

There was a pounding at the door that caused them all to start. Before they had chance to speculate, they heard a man shouting.

Rita panicked, 'Don't open it! They could be crazed!'

Saul rushed to the door. 'They need help, Rita.'

The door burst open and two hunters tumbled in to the motor home, rifles under their arms, dishevelled from a long race through the forest. One shouted, 'Where's Dennis?'

'He's right behind us,' the other replied.

Saul stood before them. 'What's going on out there?'

'It's a bloodbath,' Brad gasped.

'Goddamn Bears, that's what!' growled Ed.

Dennis jumped at the door, dragging himself on board, just as a huge paw took a swipe at him. Rita screamed. Brad pulled him out of harms way as Ed slammed the door shut.

Nick rushed to the window.

'Jesus...'

Outside, two giant bears stalked the motor home. They seemed to be covered in gravel and dirt. And there was something in their mouths.

Had they swallowed a torch? Was that fire?

They turned away from Nick, obscuring his view.

Brad gave Saul a pat on the shoulder. 'Thanks, man. You've just saved our bacon. Another few seconds and we'd have been dinner.' Saul gave Brad's shoulder a reassuring squeeze as he crossed to the kitchen unit to pour their new guests a much needed drink.

Ed sat stunned. 'Never seen bears that size before. Freaks.'

Dennis could only catch his breath.

Smugly, Rita nudged Saul, 'I told you I heard an animal!' Saul waved his wife off. He pulled up a chair for Brad.

'What's the situation, fellas?'

Brad shook his head. 'Some kind of mutant bear, disturbed by the earthquake I'll bet. At least three of them. Been chasing us down from the camp. They're smart.'

'Compared to the average bear?'

'A lot smarter. And they're hungry. Near enough had ol' Dennis here, if it weren't for the girl.'

Aimee jumped in, 'Girl?'

Brad hesitated. 'Ran out from the woods, interrupted it.' He paused as he considered his next sentence, 'I'd like to think she got away, but these things are fast. We got cut off, had to run.'

He placed his gun on the table. Aimee considered it. 'Couldn't you shoot it?'

Ed was frustrated as he tended to Dennis, 'Don't you think we tried that, missy? Hide like steel. Wouldn't go down.'

Aimee turned to Nick. He was contemplating. Hide like steel. Covered in rock and dirt. And its mouth...

'We've got to get back to the camp. She might have drawn them back there. Our friends...'

Ed cut her off, 'Girl, your friends are as good as dead. Ain't no way you can stop these things. We need to scoot. Now.'

Nick peered out of the window. 'I don't know. They've got us well covered.'

Brad joined him at the window.

The bears stalked the motor home, heads down, intent on getting to their prey.

'Like sardines.'

Brad gritted his teeth, 'Hell.'

CHAPTER 8

Sophie's blood chilled as the voices on the radio screamed. She should have turned it off, left the room, turned her attention to something else – but she couldn't. She felt guilty as she listened, trying to discern every voice.

I need to find Dad.

But the communications were garbled. Just assorted screams rising from unidentifiable sources. Frustrated, she shouted to Tyler, 'Turn it off.'

He tried to object. 'But Deputy Kevin said to...'

'Turn it off!'

Hesitantly, Tyler cut the radio off. They sat in silence. After a few moments, Sophie stood frustrated. 'I can't just sit here and listen to people die.' She considered her options, before adding, 'Can't exactly go and help, either.'

Carly looked terrified. 'What about your Dad?'

It was all Sophie could think about. But for now she had to keep a lid on her emotions. She offered Carly a reassuring smile, 'Dad'll be fine. He's got a car. He's probably on his way back here right now. Then we can all get out of here together.'

Carly nodded, placated.

Sophie turned away, hiding her concern. She pulled her cell phone from her pocket and sent her Dad a text;

'WHERE R U?'

The door burst open, Deputy Kevin and the Mayor walked in. The Mayor threw himself down in the nearest chair as Kevin sighed, 'That's everyone evacuated from out front. You kids should have gone, too.'

Sophie shook her head, 'I can't just leave my Dad. Besides, we've been manning the radio for you.'

'He would want you safe.'

'I'm not going anywhere without him.'

Kevin knew better than to argue with Hank's teenage daughter. He turned his attention to the Mayor. 'We need to get everyone else out of the park.'

The Mayor looked stunned. He muttered to himself, 'I should have listened to Hank. All those people...'

Kevin crossed to him and crouched before him. 'Mr Mayor, we need to act quickly.'

The Mayor sobbed, 'It's hopeless. So many people. They won't even know...'

Deputy Kevin stood and threw his arms up in frustration. He stormed across to the desk, ready to sweep the contents to one side in anger.

He stopped.

The Mayor blubbered.

Kevin held up a hand to silence him. They all listened intently.

The sound of a helicopter overhead.

Sophie brightened. 'Maybe it's a rescue team.'

Kevin was less optimistic. 'In one helicopter?' He listened as it drew closer. From the window, he could see it coming in to land in the now vacant parking lot out front.

He opened the door and walked out to greet it.

A man in a government issue flak jacket hurried from the helicopter, greeting Kevin halfway. The man extended a hand to Kevin, who could now read the logo on the collar of his uniform.

E.P.A – Environmental Protection Agency.

Kevin shouted over the noise of the rotor blades, 'Deputy Kevin Payton.'

'Agent Daniels. EPA.'

They both hurried towards the Ranger Station.

'Forgive me, sir. I was expecting more of you.'

Daniels smiled, 'Oh, I'm just the welcome party, Deputy. The National Guard are already en route. I'm to coordinate our response on behalf of the US Government.'

'Meaning?'

Daniels stopped and gave Kevin a twisted smile. Kevin supposed that Daniels was trying to look reassuring. 'As of now, Deputy Payton, I'm in charge.'

Daniels continued towards the Station, leaving Kevin trailing behind.

Hank's Jeep slowed as it approached an obstacle in the road. Hank was already standing, his body twisted out of the window as he brought the Jeep to a slow halt. Their windscreen had become covered in dust from their hurried escape from the geyser, which made avoiding obstacles difficult. A mile back, Hank had hit a small boulder. It should have been enough to tear right through the tyre – or worse yet, destroy the suspension. And so he had made a note to treat the road with more care, or he would be walking back to Sophie.

Lori saw a huge tree trunk blocking the path, uprooted from the last earthquake. 'Can we move it?'

'Not without a tow cable and a chainsaw.' And most of the afternoon, Hank thought. Either side, the tree hit heavy vegetation, there was no way they could even get around it.

Lori climbed out of the Jeep and they both stood assessing the situation.

'How far on foot?'

Hank squinted in the Sun and wiped his brow. 'Another couple miles.'

On cue, a roar went up in the distance. Lori could only imagine what had caused the eruption. Likely another tourist had just stumbled across those monsters...

'I don't fancy our chances.'

'Nor do I.'

She turned back to the Jeep, considering its resources. 'Can we call ahead? Send someone out to meet us?'

Hank grimaced. He'd tried to raise the Station on his way back to collect Lori. 'Radio in the Jeep is dead. Must have been the 'quake. Likely took out the radio tower.'

Lori pulled her cell phone out of her pocket. Hank did the same.

Hank looked frustrated, 'No signal.'

'Is there no way around?'

Hank shook his head. Lori could sense his frustration, his need to get back to his daughter. He suppressed it well, but she could see how close Hank was to breaking point.

'I guess there's only one place left for us,' Hank sighed.

'Avonaco?'

He nodded. 'Kevin gave him a radio. We might be able to reach the Station from up there. Or get better cell coverage.'

Lori started back toward the Jeep. Hank fidgeted angrily. She turned back to him and placed a hand on his shoulder. 'She'll be fine, Hank. She's probably long gone from the park by now.'

He nodded silently and turned back to the Jeep.

Brad watched cautiously from the window of the motor home.

The two bears sniffed at the doors and windows, sensing food inside. They stalked around the perimeter, giving it a nudge, testing the structural integrity. They grunted occasionally, as if weighing the possibilities with each other.

With each nudge, the occupants of the Motor Home gasped in horror. Saul and Rita held each other tightly. Ed braced the door and Dennis stood beside Brad, peering over his shoulder. Aimee and Nick sat huddled on the floor, clutching each other tight.

Nick whispered to Aimee, 'It's gonna be okay. They build these things to endure. There's no way they're getting in here.'

Every few minutes, the hulking shape of a bear would eclipse the sun from the kitchen window. The large shape lumbered past, its hardened fur occasionally scraping at the paintwork.

Aimee was focused on her friends Lisa and Jake, their disappearance following the first earthquake. She felt queasy, thinking of them coming across these monsters in the woods. The scream from Lisa. The blood stains that Nick found at the base of the tree.

Was it quick?

Did they suffer?

'They killed them, didn't they?' she murmured, terrified.

Nick didn't have an answer for her. He just held his girlfriend and tried not to speculate. Now was not the time. They had to survive.

Rita looked to Saul, terrified.

'I knew we should have gone to Disneyland.'

Saul gave his wife a squeeze. 'I don't know. That Mouse is on the same scale as these Bears.'

'But it doesn't eat the guests, Saul.'

He couldn't argue.

Brad continued to study the Bears through the window. 'They're learning,' he grunted.

Ed kept the door braced shut. 'Learning what?' he asked, loudly.

His friend hushed him, then continued. 'It's like they're searching for weaknesses. Weighing up the structural integrity of the thing.' He allowed himself a smile of admiration, against his better judgement. 'It's incredible.'

Saul scoffed, 'Incredible? They could tear right through this like tin foil!' He was almost hysterical and it didn't help the already tense atmosphere.

Nick growled quietly, 'Will you keep quiet. You're freaking everyone out!'

Saul opened his mouth to fire back, but as he did another jolt rocked the Motor Home.

Brad and Dennis nearly lost their balance. Ed scrambled back up the door and the rest huddled together on the floor.

Silence.

Dennis breathed, 'Okay, that was a big one.'

As he did, there was another jolt, even bigger. Cups crashed to the floor as the motor home almost tipped over. The residents skidded across the floor, hitting the furthest wall and tried to brace themselves without screaming. The motor home rocked back and forth rhythmically – the after effects of the hit.

A sizeable dent was visible in the wall from the impact.

Ed had a bad feeling. He looked around the motor home, gauging the best means of protection from the next assault. 'You ever get drunk and go cow tipping?'

He looked to Brad and Dennis, who turned away from the window, locking eyes with their friend.

'Boys, we the cow...'

Brad peered out of the window again.

He saw a bear in the distance. For a moment, he thought they had given up. And then he realised...

...the bear started to sprint towards them, head down...

Brad's eyes grew wide. He drew a sharp intake of breath as he spun from the window and shouted -

'GET DOWN!'

He jumped. Just in time. The window burst behind him from the impact of the bear. Again, the motor home rocked violently, almost tipping. The passengers were flung to the back wall, adding weight to the momentum of the tumbling motor home.

This time, the attack did not cease. The thud of approaching paws meant the second bear was readying to attack. As the motor home swung, the bear crashed in to it with tremendous force.

The motor home teetered on the brink...

...and came crashing down on its roof, overturned.

The occupants let out a scream as they toppled, crashing in to the roof along with the furniture. The windows popped from the pressure. Saul shielded his wife from the crash and Nick was knocked clear of Aimee. Brad fumbled for a rifle, but it was lost in the debris.

And the bears moved in for the kill.

A claw forced its way through the windshield,

almost grabbing Aimee's leg. She dragged herself away, screaming.

Crawling towards her, Nick pulled her aside, shielding her from harm, but a Bear was now on top of the van, the weight compressing the front of the vehicle. The drivers seat crumpled against the upturned roof as the structural integrity failed under the weight of the giant bear.

Nick screamed in pain.

His leg was underneath the drivers' seat – now trapped in the crush.

Brad scrambled over. Desperately, he looked around for any kind of tool that he could use. The kitchen table lay shattered at his feet and he grabbed at a splintered table leg. He prised it between the seat and Nick, trying to wrestle Nick free.

But he stopped dead in his tracks.

Through the window, a great snout pushed its way in to the motor home. It sniffed at its prey. Brad could feel the scalding hot breath and the mouth dripping with saliva.

Not saliva.

Something red.

Lava?

As it dripped, it scorched the upholstery. It slobbered towards Nick's prone leg and Nick swung his remaining limbs frantically, trying to fend the bear off.

Aimee tried to push forward, to help her boyfriend. Brad stopped her with an outstretched arm. 'Everyone to the back!'

Rita crawled away sobbing, Saul tried to grab for Aimee who fought against his grip. Ed fumbled with his rifle, loading it and pointing it at the bear's probing mouth. Dennis grabbed for the weapon, dragging it away from its intended target. Ed fought back, but Dennis stopped him again.

'Don't!'

The fuel tank had ruptured.

Gasoline dripped and pooled around them.

Ed understood. All it would take was one spark and it would ignite.

They had no choice.

'We have to go,' Dennis shouted through the chaos. 'Now!'

But Aimee was inconsolable. 'Nick!' she shouted, frantically.

Nick gave one last tug to free his leg. It was no use. He was bear bait. Resigned, he locked eyes with Ed. The two of them exchanged a knowing stare. Nick held out his hand and Ed gave him the rifle.

Aimee watched. 'What are you doing?'

The bear was almost frantic now, pulling at the drivers' seat furiously trying to get to its meal.

With his free hand, Nick pulled Aimee in for a final kiss.

'I love you.'

The bear was joined by his second, who could sense that his partner was close to obtaining some fresh meat. Together, they tore at the frame of the windscreen, ripping a wider hole at which they could enter.

Their claws finally tore at Nick's leg.

Saul crawled through the back window and

dragged Rita free of the wreckage. He swept his head from side to side – no bears. Hurriedly, he tried to assess their escape.

Far across the open field, he could see a dark opening.

He shouted back to the wreckage, 'There's a cave back there.'

Brad fired back, 'Then head for it!' And they ran.

Aimee tried desperately one last time to free Nick, but Brad and Dennis grabbed her by the shoulders and forced her through the back window and out in to the daylight.

As Nick winced from the pain, he found himself alone with Ed.

Ed backed away, 'You know how to use it?'

Nick knew Ed didn't have the time left to teach him. 'Go!'

Scrambling out of the back window, Ed ran for safety.

Even with everybody free and with bears ready to crunch down upon his leg, Nick found himself making one last futile attempt to free himself.

Finally, he checked the rifle.

One shot.

Saul and Rita had by now reached the mouth of the cave. Standing at the entrance, they turned back and gasped for breath as the rest of the party ran towards them.

They could see Brad signalling to them. He seemed to want them to take cover. Saul's eyes were wide. He grabbed his wife and they scrambled deeper in to the cave.

Saul could hear the screams from Aimee as she fought against Brad and Dennis. She clawed at them as they carried her in to the cave and threw her to the ground. Safely clear.

Ed was trailing behind.

'Come on!' Brad shouted in frustration. Ed sped on towards the cave.

In the motor home, tears of rage streaked Nick's face.

The nearest bear sunk its teeth deep in to his leg. His flesh burned and he screamed in agony. His blood began to pool around him, his waist grew warm and he felt close to blacking out.

With his last ounce of strength, he levelled the rifle at a pool of gasoline.

He grinned maniacally at his attackers.

'Hey, Yogi. Puts this in your picnic basket.'

Then he fired.

Brad stood just inside the cave, willing his friend on. Ed ran as fast as he could, but he was still a good distance from the cave. Brad edged out, weighing up helping his friend and staying in the safety of the cave.

'Get back!' Ed shouted and instinctively, Brad retreated in to the cave just as the motor home exploded.

Brad saw Ed make one last desperate dive towards the cave, felt the ground shudder below, the heat of the exploding petroleum hitting him in the face, stinging his eyes. As he staggered back from the blast, the cave began to crumble. Rocks dropped from the entrance, small at first but the rumble of boulders running down the outside of the cave entrance eclipsed all other noises.

Before he could react, Brad was plunged in to darkness.

Fumbling for his pocket, he found a lighter and attempted to light it as the rest of the party tried to contain their fear.

The lighter flickered to life. The entrance was sealed and Ed was outside.

Brad clawed at the rock, desperate to loosen it enough to rescue his friend, but it was useless. Behind him, Aimee was inconsolable. He turned towards her, frustrated.

Shut the fuck up! You're not the only one to have lost! Your boyfriend couldn't hold them off long enough and now he's DEAD!

Brad took a deep breath and pushed his anger and frustration to one side.

He looked to Dennis and said, matter-of-factly, 'Ed's still out there.'

Dennis trembled, 'He's gone, man.'

'He was clear of the blast. We could still reach him before those bears. If we all just calm the fuck down and start to...'

'Brad,' Dennis held his friend tight, 'We have to keep moving.'

His breathing slowed down, more controlled as he surveyed his fellow prisoners.

Aimee sobbed on Rita's shoulder. 'You left him. Why did you just leave him there? Why did you leave him?' Rita whispered to her, calming the young girl as Saul watched with a grave expression.

'I have my flashlight,' Dennis added. He fumbled with his belt and suddenly the cave was fully illuminated.

Saul met eyes with Brad, who nodded back to the old man, stoically. He took a deep breath and helped Dennis to examine the cave.

'We have a little light at least,' Brad silently wondered for how long, 'We can't dig ourselves out any time soon, this rock is too heavy. We need to find an alternative route.'

The group turned its attention toward survival.

'This cave extends back here,' Saul pointed in to a dark corner. 'Looks like a network of tunnels.'

'Good. I guess we go deeper.'

Before Brad could move on, Rita stopped him. Her voice trembled, 'What if there're more of those things down here? We're trapped!'

Brad had been trying not to consider that. Why did they think the caves would be any safer than outside?

There was a reason. Something Ed had mentioned in passing back at the camp.

'They don't like the caves,' Brad caught himself thinking out loud.

'What?' Saul asked.

'Something Ed said back at the camp. Said he'd been hunting here all his life and the bears always avoided the caves.' They had scoffed at Ed when he mentioned it.

'Why? Do they not hibernate?' Rita said.

Brad simply shrugged.

'I guess we'll find out.'

There was a much bigger question for Brad to ponder, as the group followed Dennis' flashlight deeper in to the cave -

If the bears had always avoided the caves, what the hell else was in here?

He thought of the bears outside, the rocky hide, the smell of sulphur, the heat. And the warmer the cave became, the more Brad had to stifle his fear.

CHAPTER 9

The huge metallic sign that welcomed visitors to the park rattled as the fleet of camouflaged trucks came hurtling down the road. One by one, they turned sharply on to the path leading towards the log cabin Ranger Station. Overhead, three choppers swooped towards the park in formation.

The National Guard had arrived.

But the trucks filled with troops could not distract from the main body of the military parade descending upon the park. Towards the rear of the convoy drove a large armoured RV – a Mobile Command Unit, intended as a base of operations for any crisis situation.

And behind it, being driven at a much more deliberate pace, was a large bomb. It sat cradled on the back of a truck marked 'WIDE LOAD'. Either side, yellow warning lights flashed ominously.

Very slowly, as gently as possible, the bomb was manoeuvred in to the park.

Sat watching was Agent Daniels, content that the

US Government was doing all it could to take charge of events. Slowly rising from his seat, he crossed to the porch of the Ranger Station and leaned on the pillar watching the National Guard prepare for action.

From the window, Daniels was watched by Sophie and her friends Tyler and Carly. Sophie was speechless. She had never seen so much military personnel in one place. And for what? An earthquake? It was disproportionate.

She knew that there would be a lot of people trapped in the forest – but she expected search and rescue teams. Guys with sniffer dogs and first aid kits...

Then she caught sight of the cargo. At first, it was partially obscured behind the trees. Once it emerged in to the parking lot, she let out a gasp. She turned to Deputy Kevin, who shifted anxiously in the doorway of her father's office.

'The Army?' She knew that she shouldn't take this out on Kevin – but where else could she turn now?

'They're in charge now,' Deputy Kevin muttered, helpless, 'I'm just a facilitator.'

Even Tyler couldn't contain his surprise. 'They've got a missile, dude.'

Kevin paused. Had he misheard him? 'What?' Kevin crossed to the window, his eyes wide as he gazed out at the huge bomb casing sat ready and waiting. 'Nobody said anything about a bomb.'

At that moment, Agent Daniels burst through the door, a group of men in army uniform trailing behind him. He indicated towards the meeting room and they barged through. Sophie noticed radio equipment and rolls of paper in their arms – they looked like topographical maps of the area.

Kevin stood before Daniels and puffed out his chest. 'Agent Daniels, why is there a missile in my park?'

Daniels stood looking deep in to Kevin's eyes, an amused expression on his face. Sophie recognised it as the look of a man who has taken on much bigger fish. Daniels was amused by Kevin.

As if to confirm her suspicions, Daniels' next words were calculated, almost patronising. 'Just a precaution at this stage, Deputy. We need to be prepared for any and all eventualities. Now be a pal and sort out some coffee for my men? I'd be obliged.'

Kevin was unmoved. 'To bring a weapon like that in to a National Park...'

'You have an objection, Deputy?'

'It's wrong,' Kevin squirmed.

'How so?'

Kevin considered. 'Morally.'

Daniels let out a long, derisive laugh then slapped a reassuring hand on Kevin's arm. It was as good as patting him on the head and ruffling his hair. He grinned as he said, 'Morally wrong? Son, let Uncle Sam decide what's morally right or wrong. What we need is a concerted effort to stop those bears from slaughtering any more innocent people. Is that understood?'

Silence.

With a wink, Daniels sauntered away, leaving Deputy Kevin flustered and embarrassed. He looked to Sophie, who offered him nothing. She wondered how her father might have handled the situation. He was the type of man who didn't take commands lightly. He was often in dispute with the Mayor or with the County. They admired his resolve and treated him with the respect that they felt he had earned. She could not help but feel her father would have been disappointed.

He stood on a rocky outcrop.

Behind him, his small log cabin home. Before him, the beauty of the park laid out before him. Usually so peaceful, so serene. It was why he moved here. To embrace his heritage, seek enlightenment, be at one with nature.

He closed his eyes.

The All Mother whispered her displeasure.

Her anger, her disappointment, her resentment – he could feel it all and the rage welled up inside of him. His stomach turned from the intensity, the strength of feeling. In waves, her vengeance washed over him and he pulled back.

A gasp, eyes open.

Now he understood.

He looked out across the park. There was a few small plumes of smoke trailing in to the sky. He wondered if it was Them or if the people were fighting back. He could hear screams echo across the valley below and in the far distance was engines and rotorblades and soldiers.

This would not end well.

Above, an Eagle soared majestically, surveying the carnage below. It came to land, resting on a rock not far from him. The Eagle turned to him, looked him long and hard in the eye.

'I'm sorry,' he told the Eagle.

It seemed to nod before spreading its wings and flying far from the park. He watched as it became a speck on the horizon and was eventually gone.

Then the Jeep came rolling up the dirt path, stopping at the cabin behind him. He heard the doors open, the two occupants step out and move toward him. 'Avon,' the visitor called. It was Hank.

Avon strolled back to greet them. Hank was trembling with worry. Lori was covered in dirt and looked exhausted. Hank approached Avon purposefully, 'I need to use your radio.'

'It's quite the scene down there, Hank.' Avon struggled to keep his lip from trembling. He blinked away some tears, 'So much pain and suffering'

Hank continued, 'Road's out. I need to check in with Kevin.'

'Strangers have arrived. I can hear them. They bring great destruction. They are making Her angry.'

'Enough of the cryptic crap, all right?' Hank exploded, 'There are bears down there. Some kind of prehistoric throwback. I saw them with my own eyes. They're huge, thick hide and deep red eyes. I know, it sounds crazy, but it's true.' He hesitated. 'They're killing people.'

Avon nodded, gravely. 'The All Mother is angry.'

'Yeah, well so is the Sheriff,' Hank said, dismissively. He tried to control himself, storming off towards Avon's cabin with Lori in tow.

They sat in Avon's parlour, Hank huddled over the radio as Lori fidgeted nervously. Hank bashed angrily at the buttons on the radio, shouting in to the microphone repeatedly, 'Deputy Payton, this is the Sheriff, come in.'

There was only static.

'Kevin, are you there? Over.'

No reply.

'Can anybody here me? Please respond, over.' Hank became more and more frustrated. Lori sympathised. More than anything, Hank wanted to check on his daughter. She checked her cell phone again. Avon smiled.

'Never any signal up here, even on a good day.'

Lori sounded disappointed. Avon gave her a reassuring smile.

'Most of the time, that's exactly how I like it. Helps me connect with Nature. No distractions.'

She nodded politely. Hank rolled his eyes.

Avon hesitated, then continued, 'Your Sheriff here, never much cared for Native American prophecy. I get tourists up here a couple times a week, they like to hear my stories, see some of the sights. Course, I'm always happy to show them.' He averted his gaze, staring at the floor deep in lament, 'There's not many of us left who practice the old religions. Whether people believe them or not, it's nice to pass on some of the old proverbs.'

And make sure She is protected. We're so dangerously close this time. She is furious.

'Do you live up here alone?' Lori asked.

'I like to think of it as peaceful solitude. Besides, I have Spirit for company.' He hadn't seen Spirit for days. Was this the reason? He couldn't think about it right now...

Lori was intrigued. 'Spirit?'

Hank grunted, 'His pet bear.'

'It's not a pet.'

Lori's eyes grew wide. 'You have a bear?'

Avon sat forward in his chair, 'He's wild. But he watches out for me, and I for him,' he said, reassuringly. 'He's a spiritual guide, hence the name.'

Lori thought back to the geyser. The giant bear with the fiery eyes, bounding towards her on all four legs. The speed, the intensity, the body heat. It made her shiver with fear. 'Aren't you ever afraid he might attack you?'

'All the time,' Avon laughed, 'I should be, he's a bear! But in fear, there is a respect. He knows that. He knows he could snap me in half like a twig, but he chooses not to do it. At least, not yet. And for that, I'm grateful. It's a respect of Nature, something which your Sheriff likes to forget every hunting season.'

Hank snorted, 'I don't forget, Avon. I just do my job.'

'How many men have said that over the years. Look where we are now.'

Hank threw the radio down, 'Not today, Avon. I'm really not in the mood. We've got people trapped out there and my daughter...' Hank couldn't finish his sentence. He picked up the radio and continued to attempt contact.

'I'm sorry, Hank,' Avon offered, 'But we need to proceed with caution. What's happening out there is the Great Hunt. The die has been cast and we have to act rationally, or they'll slaughter us all. Mankind is on the menu.'

Lori looked confused. 'You make it sound as if this could have been prevented.'

'Back when my people used to farm the land, they used to tell the tale of the All Mother - what you might refer to as Mother Nature. According to the stories of my tribe, the All Mother was a person. She walked amongst us, offered advice and wisdom. Not in the form of a woman, but in the form of a Great Bear. Under her protection, the tribe had food, warmth, shelter. She sacrificed herself knowingly, because the tribe would use every part of her to survive and it pleased her. In return, my tribe built totems, they prayed to her, they even built a Temple – a means to always communicate, to seek truth, wisdom, even forgiveness.'

Avon indicated towards a small totem that stood in the corner of the room. At the top, the face of a grizzly bear with its mouth wide open in mid growl. It was carved beautifully. Lori studied it as Avon continued.

'When our lands were taken from us, the All Mother watched on. She wasn't troubled, because she knew she would always provide, no matter how bad things got for us. Some of the tribe, they didn't understand. They thought the All Mother had abandoned our people, they became riddled with doubt, they left the tribe. My family always stayed true. One day, my Great Grandfather came across an Old Bear, laying on the floor of the forest. Some hunters had chased it down, killed it for sport. They'd done nothing with the body. They hadn't taken the skin, the meat, hadn't even claimed a trophy. They had killed it because it was there - just so that they could say, 'I've killed a bear'

'My Great Grandfather fell to his knees before the animal and he wept. As his tears dampened the fur of the great beast a voice spoke to him. The All Mother. She told him of her anger, that man had become greedy and spiteful, that her offerings were rejected. She resented the giving of flesh for man to boast of meagre achievements and she vowed to stop. She told him the day would come when she would accept the sacrifice of man – that the price of her flesh would be redeemed in the blood of man.'

Avon paused. Lori was engrossed, her heart heavy. Hank shook his head in frustration. Avon simply grinned and without turning to Hank said, 'I can sense that look, Hank,' and laughed. Lori saw it too, the disdain on Hank's face for old folk stories.

She had to ask, 'Is it true?'

Avon threw his hands up, 'Who can say? It makes for a beautiful story. And my Great Grandfather believed every word that he said when he repeated it to the tribe. Until now, I've told it to tourists as a proverb - 'beware the greed of man'. But today? Today, things are different,' he said ominously.

Together, they say for a few moments, reflecting on the story. Hank interrupted the silence, 'I can't reach anyone on this damned thing. I don't know if the power's out or what.'

'Maybe they're concentrating on relief efforts,' Lori offered, 'Could be there's no one to man the comms.'

Hank pondered this and then jumped to his feet. 'Either way, we need to get moving. You have any guns up here?'

Avon shook his head.

'Any weapons at all?'

Silence.

'It's gonna be a long walk back without some form

of protection. That pet of yours gets our scent and we're food.'

Spirit missing. Earthquakes. Bear attacks.

The whispering on the wind.

She was angry.

Avon stood determined. 'Hank, I think you should trust me.'

'What are you thinking?' Hank asked cautiously.

'You guys can't get back to the Station, right?'

'Not without a long trek on foot. But if that's what we have to do...' It was suicide and Hank knew it. The journey would take hours and there would be no way they could avoid an attack.

'So you're stuck up here with the crazy old hermit.' There was a gleam in Avon's eyes.

Hank sighed, 'Avon, if you're planning any...'

'About a mile from here is my tribe's temple. The shrine to the All Mother.'

Hank threw his hands up in exasperation. He paced across the room. 'Come on, Avon. This isn't the time for your hokey tribal stuff. My daughter's out there. We've got innocent people trapped in this park.'

But Avon was determined. 'And from up here, there's not a damn thing you can do about it.'

Hank stopped. He looked to Lori, hoping she might see sense. Instead she shrugged, 'He's got a point.'

Avon approached Hank, held his shoulders between his arms and pleaded with him, 'Maybe there's more to this old fable than you think.'

'Like what?' Hank was unmoved.

'I want to go to the shrine, pray to the All Mother...'

Hank was dumbfounded. He started to rage, banged his fist against the wall in frustration as Lori tried to settle him.

'...If the stories are true, then we may be able to satiate her desires, send the Bears back where they came from.'

Lori managed to calm Hank. He stood staring at Avon, perplexed. 'Are you serious?'

Even Lori had to admit that Avon may be right. 'You saw those things, Hank. Did you believe in giant prehistoric bears before today?'

'That's not the point.'

Avon folded his arms, defiantly, 'I'm going to the shrine, Hank. As Park Ranger, you can either accompany me or you can sit here and wait for rescue. Knowing what's out there, I'd say it's better to do something, however crazy you think it is, than do nothing.'

The room was silent. Avon's determination had won over Lori, but Avon could almost hear Hank's inner conflict as he struggled to justify this.

Hank's head throbbed.

Could he get to Sophie by car?

No, there was no other route from here to the Ranger Station.

Could he get to her on foot?

Not without a four hour trek, and that was if he could avoid a mangling at the hands of the bears.

Could he get a message through?

The radio wasn't responding. There was nothing he could do to fix it.

Sit here and wait for this to blow over.

Follow Avon – at the very least, keep him from getting killed.

He hesitated. 'I'll drive.'

Avon laughed, 'You think my people had four by four's when they built that shrine? There's no road, Hank. We go on foot.' He crossed to his bookshelf and took down a few essential books and began to pack some rations.

Lori pulled Hank to one side and whispered, 'You don't have to do this. You can try and contact the Station. I'll bring him straight back once he's done.'

Hank grimaced, 'No, it's okay. He's right, there's nothing we can do from here but sit and wait. I'd rather keep myself occupied than wait for a rescue.'

Stood at the door, bag packed, was Avon. He stuffed a large ceremonial hunting knife in to his belt.

'Ready?'

Hank nodded, 'Let's go.'

CHAPTER 10

Brad's eyes were adjusting to the lack of light as they continued down the cave tunnels. With only Dennis' light flickering at the front of their party, Brad brought up the rear. Ahead, Saul helped his wife navigate the uneven floor with a reassuring hand on her elbow. Aimee walked silently, disconnected from the party – still in shock at the loss of her partner, the bears, the attack, the explosion -

Which brought Brad's thoughts back to Ed, trapped on the outside. Would they have heard his screams through the fallen rock?

He shivered.

'Hold on,' Dennis shouted from the front of the group. He had stopped and was examining the cave wall.

Something hung there.

Brad eased his way past Saul and Rita, joining his friend, who pointed the flashlight up at the hangings.

A rack of old oil lanterns, covered in cobwebs.

Saul reached for one, prising it from its moorings.

'Well, at least we ain't the first people to ever come down this way,' Brad offered.

Saul pondered, 'Could it be some sort of mine?'

'Could be. Here, give me a hand with these. Let's see if we can get 'em working.' Brad fidgeted in his pockets for his lighter as Saul checked the torch for oil.

Rita took this as a good moment to get some rest. She sat herself on a rock next to Aimee. The young girl wore a blank expression. She was in shock. Rita tried to encourage her to talk. With a nudge, she asked, 'How are you holding up, sweetheart?'

Aimee was slow to respond. 'I don't know. I can't stop thinking about Nick. We'd been together since High School.' Her voice cracked, she stopped and collected her thoughts. Rita sat patiently. After a few minutes, Aimee began, 'It was me that convinced him to come on this trip. He wanted to go somewhere else, just the two of us. Something more romantic. But I just... I was frightened.'

Rita listened quietly, waited for Aimee to go on.

'He'd been talking about the future, making plans, talking about getting a place. I guess I thought if we were alone together then he might do something like propose.'

Rita squeezed Aimee's hand. 'Would that have been such a bad thing?'

Aimee slowly shook her head, 'I just didn't feel ready. So I convinced him to come on a stupid spring break camping trip, just have fun without the pressure of being an adult or thinking about the future. I guess I was just being selfish.'

Saul continued to struggle with the oil lantern. Rita couldn't help but smile. She stroked Aimee's arm. 'You can't dwell on things, sweetheart. Me and Saul, we've been together fifty years. Most of that time, we've spent it with our kids, our grandkids. You spend so much of your life looking after everyone else, you feel selfish when you decide to do something for yourself for once, to branch out. I knew when Saul retired I wanted us to get away, see some sights, leave our old lives behind us while we can. The kids are all grown up, they don't need us hanging around any more. So here we are, on the trip of a lifetime.'

They both considered for a few minutes. Rita scoffed, 'Some trip, huh?' And paused. 'I just keep thinking to myself; maybe we should have stayed at home. We wouldn't be in this mess.'

She looked across the cavern and watched Saul working feverishly with Brad. 'Then I see Saul, trying to manage a crisis. I see a life in him that I haven't seen in years. And part of me is glad that we're here. We may have lost Nick, but we saved you. And we're all going home. No one else gets hurt. No one.'

Aimee rested her head on Rita's shoulder. She was exhausted.

After a few moments, Saul let out a cheer as he lit an oil lamp. He lifted it up triumphantly, turning to his wife with glee in his eyes. They shared a loving look, absolute trust in each other. Saul sheepishly turned back to Brad.

'How's about that, huh? Think we can get a few of these going?'

Dennis then lit another lamp in the far corner and with the shadows retreating he found an old workbench. Amongst the dust, several artefacts lay on the table.

'Hey, I think this might be an old Gold Mine,' he called out, examining the objects on the table.

Brad joined him, 'Found something?'

He nodded. There was a scroll. Carefully, Dennis unravelled it and placed a stone on each corner as he spread it out across the workbench.

Together, Dennis and Brad studied it.

'Looks like there's a track down one of these tunnels,' Dennis traced his finger down the line.'

'Must be for a mine cart,' Brad added.

Dennis traced the end of the track, tapping his finger on an exit point. 'Comes out on the side of this hill, here.'

Brad looked closer. In the corner of his eye, he could see the look on Rita's face. The expectation of rescue, that this tunnel definitely provided a way out. He didn't want to risk the disappointment. 'How do we know that entrance still exists? This stuff is pretty old.'

'You got any better ideas?'

He did not.

Saul joined them. He had found some equipment in the opposite corner of the cavern. He handed Brad a pickaxe. 'These might come in handy.'

Brad nodded, swinging the pickaxe in one hand. The wood was rotting and the pick itself was rusty, but it had enough life in it for now – for their purpose, anyway. He turned to address the group. 'Okay, if we find this track, we can follow it right through the mine, should bring us out about half a mile from where we came in. Let's carry as much of this equipment as we can.'

Collectively, they rose and began to gather any supplies they could find.

Dennis used his oil lamp to guide him. His gaze

settled upon a row of barrels. Breaking the first one open, he looked inside. His breathing stopped. He looked across at Brad and beckoned him silently over.

'What you got?'

Dennis indicated to the barrel.

Lifting his torch, Brad peered inside.

Dynamite. Bundles of it. Still dry.

'Holy shit,' Brad whispered.

He looked around to check no one could overhear him, then pulled Dennis in close. He whispered in his ear, 'Carry as much as you can. If any of those bears show up, we'll give them something to chew on.'

Silently, Dennis nodded.

Brad turned away, joining the rest of the crew as Dennis carefully filled his bag.

Loaded up, they headed deeper in to the tunnels.

When Deputy Kevin stepped in to the meeting room, he was surprised to see the room had become a command centre. Sat around the table, like a scene from Dr Strangelove, the uniformed personnel pored over a map of the park which was spread across the table. Small markers were being pushed around as they considered strategic positions and Kevin couldn't help but laugh. Do they carry these little toys around with them? Weren't there more important things to bring?

At the far end of the room, the Mayor sat silently rubbing his temples. Agent Daniels loomed over the table, clearly in charge. Next to him, a Sergeant explained the plan.

Kevin looked for somewhere to sit, but all the seats were taken. Instead, he squeezed past a few men and peered over Daniels shoulder as he listened.

'...Our concern is that any increase in seismic activity could unleash more of these things upon the park. To that end, we have devised a plan to deliver a payload via the geyser that will hopefully mend any fissures caused by the earthquakes. Our team will move in to position here...'

The markers were repositioned on the map. Right on to the geysers.

Wasn't that where Sheriff Hank was?

'...setting up a Command Unit on the perimeter. The warhead will be rigged to drill through the geyser...'

Payload.

Warhead.

Drill.

Kevin jumped in, 'I'm sorry, the what?'

The Sergeant stopped, 'Warhead.'

'You're going to blow up the geyser?' Kevin was irate.

The Mayor grumbled from the corner, 'Don't worry, Deputy. It won't ruin the aesthetics of your park. Just let my men get to work.'

My men. It made Daniels shoot the Mayor a look, who then avoided his gaze.

Kevin continued, 'Aesthetics are not my concern, Mr Mayor. You want to calm the seismic activity by blowing it up?' He was stunned.

The Sergeant took a breath, 'We're hoping the exposure to radiation will fuse some of that rock back together.'

Hoping.

Kevin jumped, 'Radiation?'

'Is there an echo in here?' Daniels started, angrily, 'Deputy, we have a lot to get through, so...' Daniels tried to usher Kevin out of the room.

The Sergeant was angry at the interruption and turned to front Kevin. 'What the hell else would a nuclear warhead do?'

Shrugging the guiding hand of Daniels away, Kevin stared at the men horrified. Why was everybody so happy with this? He shouted, 'You're going to nuke the goddamn park?!'

'We'll detonate as deep as we can, to minimise the damage up top,' the Sergeant offered, matter-of-fact.

'But there are people out there.'

The Mayor looked up, his eyes red. 'Son, anyone who's out there is already dead,' he said gravely.

'Sheriff Walker is out there.'

'God rest his soul...' the Mayor muttered.

Kevin shook his head. His breathing was erratic. 'No, I... I can't let you do this.'

Daniels reaffirmed his grip on Kevin's arm. Through gritted teeth he excused himself for a moment as he dragged Kevin to the door of the meeting room. The rest of the room chattered amongst themselves as Daniels spoke in a deliberate tone to Kevin. 'Perhaps I didn't make myself clear when I arrived. This site is now classed as a disaster area. The containment efforts are under my control.'

He pointed a large accusatory finger at Kevin's face, 'Your remit as Park Ranger is to pick up the trash and help cats out of trees, not to involve yourself in military operations. Have I made myself clear?'

Silence.

Agent Daniels swung the door open to escort Kevin out.

In the reception area, Sophie looked up. She watched Kevin, his face pleading.

'If you go through with this, you'll kill more people than the bears ever will.'

'Those people out there are already dead,' Daniels spat.

'You can't know that for certain.'

Daniels shoved his finger in to the chest of the Deputy, prodding at him aggressively. 'I can know that, Deputy. The United States Government has ordered containment and extermination. Anybody still alive out there is considered expendable.'

Kevin stutters, 'It's barbaric.'

'It's for the good of the country, Deputy.'

They paused, Daniels waiting for Kevin to walk away. Kevin looks across the room to Sophie, her father still lost out in the wilderness, now no chance of survival. 'And what if it doesn't work? What if it doesn't mend the tectonic plates like you think it will?'

Daniels shrugs, 'Then hopefully it'll take out enough of those big bastards for us to get a handle on this crisis.'

Kevin stared at Sophie, who watched him with a look of concern. He knew she couldn't hear the conversation, but he could see she had a sense as to how well this was going. He indicated towards Sophie. 'You want me to go out there and tell Sophie that you've killed her father?'

He scoffed. 'I want you to do your job, Deputy. If you disobey my orders, I'll have you thrown in a cell and you can watch this park go up in smoke through your goddamn bars. How's that sound?' The sick smile on Daniels face only riled Kevin further. He thought about throwing a punch, but what good would that do? He realised his fists were clenched, his muscles tensing.

Sophie stood up, about to come over.

Kevin took a deep breath, holding himself back.

Daniels just smirked and backed away. 'Sergeant, please continue,' he instructed as he shut the door of the meeting room in Kevin's face.

In a rage, Kevin ran to Sheriff Hank's office and slammed the door shut behind him. He wanted to scream. He wanted to tear the shelves down and swipe everything from the table in anger.

He needed Hank.

Hank would know what to do.

He tried the radio one last time. Nothing. He stifled a cry. Maybe he wasn't cut out to be a Park Ranger after all. But who could be in these circumstances?

Shortly, Sophie and her friend Tyler joined Kevin in the meeting room. After some coaxing, Kevin told them the whole plan, for better or for worse.

Sophie was incensed.'They're gonna do what?!'

'They wouldn't listen. I tried to stop them.'

Sophie struggled to breath. Her father was alive. She knew he was. He was a survivor. But a *nuclear bomb*?!

He didn't know. He was out there alone and didn't know what was coming.

'We've got to do something.'

'I've been trying to contact your Dad, tell him to get the hell out of there. There's no radio signal.'

'And my cell phone is out,' Sophie added, 'earthquake must have brought down the tower, or something. He won't see this coming. Who the hell would?'

Kevin tried to reassure her, 'I'll sort this out. I'll stall them, or...'

'Leave it to us,' Tyler said.

'You?' Kevin was surprised. He had forgotten Tyler was even there. What could he possibly do?

Tyler smiled, 'You think we've never protested the military before? Dude, nothing gets under their skin like a teenager.'

Kevin shook his head, vehemently. 'I can't let you guys do this. I promised Hank...'

Sophie stopped him. 'The only thing that matters now is stopping that warhead and saving my Dad,' she said. 'There's no way you're going to stop me,' she added, resolutely.

Kevin considered.

With their meeting now complete and everyone

fully briefed, Agent Daniels stepped outside for some air. His troops rushed around the parking lot, preparing for manoeuvres. He certainly appreciated military precision. It was days like this that made him glad to be a government agent. Environmental Protection could be so dull at times...

He strolled across to the lorry that carried the bomb. As he passed the shell casing, he reached out and silently caressed it. When he reached the cab at the front, the driver leaned out of his window awaiting instructions.

'I've already sent a crew on ahead to clear the road,' Daniels told him. 'Should be plain sailing from here. Rendezvous with Mobile Command and start setting up. I'll meet you there. Understood?'

The driver nodded. Daniels stepped back and the lorry pulled away.

Daniels watched the bomb go. A tarpaulin partially obscured it from the rear – something he had not noticed on its arrival.

And he thought he saw something move underneath it.

Just the wind.

He turned away just as Sophie peered out from the back of the lorry.

She was on her way.

CHAPTER 11

Lori couldn't help but enjoy the serenity afforded at this end of the park, despite the chaos down below. She had never ventured this far before. Avon was leading them through the most beautiful landscape she had ever encountered. The sun was high, the green of the large trees was varied and impressive. The trail they followed was overgrown from lack of use but not inaccessible.

It was serene. A rare piece of tranquillity. She hoped that she could come back here some time and fully explore. The air was so fresh, the stream they followed was so clear. It trickled towards a much larger river and Lori focused upon the sound of the running water.

Very soon, the running water was replaced by a great rush.

They came upon the end of the river. A great waterfall with exotic greenery lapping at the shores. From this height, it was hard to see the base of the waterfall through the mist that was thrown up.

But it was beautiful.

And set across the waterfall, clearly a forgotten tourist route, was a long rope suspension bridge.

Hank stopped in front on it.

'Are we close?' Lori asked.

'Once we've crossed the falls, we just follow the trail down in to the valley,' Avon said.

'It's beautiful.'

Avon smiled. 'That's why I stay here.'

In that moment, she understood Avon's belief in Mother Nature – the All Mother, he called Her – and his need to protect the park around him. Whilst Hank was a Park Ranger, his job was far more geared towards accommodating tourists. What Avon did, it was a calling...

'I'm surprised they let you stay here. National Parks can be a bit precious.' She shot a glance at Hank. Unintentional, but she couldn't help but feel some level of resentment that he could not appreciate Avon's love for the park.

'They get enough work out of me in return.'

Hank gave the old Native American a wink. 'Still can't get you in to this uniform, though.'

'I don't need a badge to show I care, Hank.' Sensing Hank's wounded pride, Avon added, 'Besides, green just isn't my colour.'

Avon took a step on to the bridge, grabbing the rope for support as it creaked and swayed slightly from under use.

He stopped.

His ears pricked.

Lori watched him. Avon was listening, his eyes closed. She turned to Hank, who had frozen still. He was also watching Avon and was now struggling to listen to whatever it was Avon had heard.

A whisper on the wind. Her calling.

A rustle.

The bushes behind them?

Lori couldn't bear the silence any longer. 'What is it?' she asked, suddenly alert.

Avon shook his head, 'How could I have been so foolish...'

He did not answer Lori, who turned her attention back to Hank. His eyes were darting back from where they had come – the path leading through the forest back to Avon's Cabin.

'Can you hear something?' he asked Lori. She listened.

Nothing.

Then the trees shuddered, ever so slightly.

'They know where we're heading,' Avon sounded tense. 'They're trying to stop us.' He cursed himself in a language that Lori did not know.

'How can they know where we're heading? They're bears!' Hank hissed.

Avon indicated to the trees. 'Tell that to our hunters.'

And suddenly, Lori heard a snort. The bushes parted and two large bears slowly stalked out towards them. It was the closest she had been since the geyser and a pang of fear tore at her insides. But up close, she was able to scrutinise them like she hadn't before.

Their rocky hides shifted with their hulking muscles as they sauntered towards them and Lori finally realised – they weren't caked in rock, or rubble, or mud.

Their hides were rock. Shifting rock. And beneath the razor sharp contours that substituted for bristles, she could see an orangey glow. It pulsed through their muscles. Not blood.

Magma?

It might explain the heat that their bodies gave off, that molten smell that accompanied the bears.

The eyes. Those red, hate filled eyes. Burning with fire.

Their hungry mouths dripping with molten saliva.

They had been awoken from the earthquake. Some kind of mutant Magma Bear. She immediately wondered how much of Avon's story was true. Were these sent by the All Mother? He said she was angry...

All of this in a split second, before Lori blurted, 'We've got to get out here.'

Hank slowly backed away. The Magma Bears had not yet attacked. Why? What were they waiting for? No time to stick around and find out -

'The bridge,' Hank instructed, and the three of them darted on to it as the bears pounced, their sharp claws missing them by inches. Lori stood between Avon and Hank, squeezing her between them, trying to protect her. She fought her way out of their grip. She didn't want protecting.

From behind Hank, she could see the two magma bears stalking at the edge of the cliff. She noted how narrow the bridge was, how Avon, Hank and her were stood single file. The bears couldn't get across a bridge this narrow.

But they knew this. She could see it in their eyes.

One of the bears let out a terrible roar, long and pronounced. Lori presumed it was a roar of frustration, but it didn't take her long to be proven wrong.

'That was close.'

Avon grunted, 'We're not clear yet.'

Lori looked to the opposite side. A third magma bear now stood blocking their exit. The roar was a signal. The bears had contained their prey. The bear drooled, its teeth shown – almost a grin.

On either side, the bears stood patiently.

They were trapped.

'They've been toying with us,' Avon was frustrated.

'What now?' Hank asked.

'I don't know.'

Suddenly, Lori was thrown off balance. She clung desperately to the coarse rope, burning the palm of her hand as she struggled to maintain her balance. She saw that one of the bears had extended a paw on to the bridge, testing the wood's strength. The wooden beams creaked, the rope audibly tightened.

The bridge shook.

They smelt burning.

The bear lifted his paw away, a partial retreat. The wood was charred where his paw had fallen.

'It won't take their weight,' Avon noted.

'Or their heat,' Lori added.

Hank's eyes darted around. He leaned over the side of the bridge, looking deep in to the basin of the waterfall. 'Looks like we're taking a short cut to the bottom of this valley.'

Avon panicked, 'A shortcut?' He leaned over, following Hank's gaze. Lori watched as Avon tried to judge the distance from the bridge to the water below. He had made up his mind.

'We have to jump.'

'Jump?' Lori shrieked, 'Are you crazy? The fall could kill us!' She was not the adventurous sort. She shunned the outdoors until an interest in seismology added a healthy bronze to her skin. There was no way she could jump this. She wasn't even sure she still remembered how to swim!

'It's deep enough. Trust me.'

She hesitated, weighing her options. Maybe the bears would get bored and leave?

Or maybe Avon was right. Maybe they knew. Maybe they were trying to stop them. How long could a magma bear hold out for a meal?

'Fuck!' she shouted, in frustration.

Avon grabbed her hand and held it tight. They locked eyes.

The bears shook the bridge again. A few loose boards at either end gave way. The rope started to strain.

Avon helped her keep her balance.

With a last calming glance, Lori stepped over the guide rope. Her heart raced and she tried to control her breathing.

One last deep breath.

She jumped.

Lori fell for an eternity. She thought of the alternatives, the claws and teeth of the hungry magma bears piercing her flesh. The scolding heat from their volcanic blood.

She felt a freezing shock, the breath knocked from her. Lori sank deep underwater, and she couldn't stop. She felt as though she had fallen twice as long underwater than above and she had to force herself from panicking.

Her momentum stopped, natural buoyancy winning out. She rose to the surface, gasping for air.

She was safe.

Lori shouted up to Avon and Hank, then scrambled to the shore.

Above her, Hank watched in horror. The landing looked rough.

'Hank,' Avon prompted.

'No way.'

'Hank, you have to start trusting me.'

Another jolt. This time a rope gave way. It snapped back, narrowly avoiding Hank's ear as it swooped by. So close.

The bridge lulled to one side and Hank could feel himself beginning to topple. One more jolt and this bridge would overturn.

Avon continued, his arms tense as he held himself upright, 'I know this is all a stretch for you, Hank. The fables, the prophecy... but these bears have chased us here for a reason.'

Hank tried to ignore him, tried to find an alternative route out of this. Why had he come? He should have tried to get back to the Ranger Station.

Avon made one last try, 'If we let them stop us now,' he shouted, 'you can kiss your daughter goodbye.'

But he had already done that when he turned his back on the trek back to the Station. This was it. This was the end. 'You go,' he told Avon, turning to face the bears stoically. 'I'll hold them off.'

Avon hesitated briefly, then stood back to back with Hank.

'What are you doing?' Hank shouted.

The bears were now gnawing at the rope. It singed, ready to snap.

'If you won't come with me, then I guess we both die together.'

'Are you crazy?'

'So you always tell me!' Avon barked.

The bridge warped violently.

Hank was left with no choice. He turned to Avon and grabbed him tight. 'Aw, what the Hell...'

- and with a shout, they both jumped together from the bridge, seconds before it collapsed. As the ropes swung back, the weight of the wooden beams forced the bridge to smash against the side of the cliff face.

Lori watched from the bank as both men tumbled through the air and splashed in to the basin of the waterfall. She waited a few seconds, concerned.

Suddenly, they both sprung up from the water, cheering and whooping hysterically. Slowly, they swam towards the embankment and Lori offered them a hand as they dragged themselves on to land.

Hank lay exhausted and exhilarated on the grass.

Avon sat himself down next to Hank and grinned.

'Maybe we should start adding this to the tour?'

By the light of the old oil lanterns, the group had managed to find the mine cart track and were now making good speed walking beside it. Brad considered how lucky they had been to have found enough oil to light the lanterns. With the flashlight, they couldn't have made it this far. They didn't even see the workbench or tools in the cavern until the oil lamps were lit.

Which then made him wonder why exactly so much had been left down here in an abandoned mine. Ed knew the bears avoided the mine – even the miners seemed quick to leave it...

It was best to push it to the back of his mind, turning his attention back to the task at hand.

Aimee walked between Saul and Rita.

'You think they really mined for gold down here?' she asked.

Saul seemed confident. 'For sure,' he said, 'at least until the Civil War. My family came over hear during the Gold Rush. My Great Grandfather used to pan for gold. Can you imagine that?' He chuckled to himself. 'Made a good living of it, too. The fortyniners, they called them back then.'

Aimee surveyed the cave walls. 'You think there's any more left in these tunnels?'

'Could be.,' Saul replied. 'Whoever was down here sure left in a hurry.'

Brad found himself brought back to that foreboding question. Why did they leave?

'You think they found something?' Dennis asked, referring to some hidden danger.

Saul shook his head, trying to expel the thought from his own mind. 'I sure hope not. I'd like to see some daylight before too long. I feel like a mole down here.' He paused, reminded of a funny story from his childhood. He thought it might lighten the mood. 'You know, when I was a young lad, me and a few friends, we...'

But Saul absentmindedly walked in to Brad, who had stopped with his arms outstretched – preventing the group from walking any further. Saul was pulled from his reverie immediately.

Rita looked on. 'Are we stopping?'

'I don't think we have a choice,' Brad replied as he crouched down, staring at something below him. There was silence. Nobody moved. Rita grew impatient.

'Well, what is it?'

Dennis pushed his way forward to join his friend. He crouched down beside Brad and took a sharp intake of breath. 'I guess we found out why the fortyniners were in a hurry to leave.'

Brad was staring in to a large chasm underneath the mine cart track. The track carried on across the hole, undisturbed. But the rock underneath had loosened and revealed a huge chamber. Brad supposed the miners didn't know about it. They had cut the tunnel inches above it, unaware of the danger below.

The chamber was illuminated by a bright red glow and a few scattered flames. As his eyes adjusted, Brad realised this was lava. A whole stream of hot, flowing lava.

'Christ, how deep can we be?' Dennis supposed.

'Could be we're on a fault line, like San Francisco. Would explain those 'quakes we've been experiencing.' Brad continued to stare in to the lava chamber. He could swear he saw something move.

The licking of the flames, something casting a dancing shadow across the rock wall.

Then he saw them. Unmoving, but definitely there.

Laying either side of the river of lava – huge sleeping bears, the kind that had attacked them up top. Rocky. Burning. This explained things.

He tried to count them, but there were so many. He scanned their hulking bodies.

At least a hundred.

By this time, the entire group stood hunched around him, examining the chasm.

'Great,' Saul cried, 'We escape the bears by walking right in to their den!'

Aimee's voice cracked as she turned to Brad, 'I thought you said the bears avoided the cave.'

It made sense now. 'The regular bears, not these...Volcano Bears!'

'The normal bears knew something we didn't,' Aimee added. 'They've been avoiding them ever since this mine collapsed.'

Brad sighed.

'No wonder the earthquake woke them up,' Saul exclaimed. 'Lying that close to molten rock. They're taking a nap right on the fault line!'

Saul was right. These were some kind of mutants, for sure. And the recent activity had caused them to go wandering. But the few that Brad had seen around the park had nothing on the numbers still slumbering. They needed to be careful.

'What now?' Dennis asked.

'We've got to turn back,' Rita cried, 'There's no way across there.'

Brad shook his head. 'Map didn't show any other way to the exit.'

They considered. 'We could wait for rescue back by the entrance?' Dennis offered.

'Knowing that these bears are asleep right below us? We've got to press on,' said Brad as he shined his oil lamp around the walls, looking for a solution.

The tracks were thin and slippery, they couldn't tightrope walk across them. But at the edges of the tunnel wall, he could see a small rocky ledge. It certainly didn't look safe, but it was their only means across. If they all hugged the wall, they could sidestep across the chasm one by one.

'There's a path,' Brad told them. 'It's small, but we can get across.'

He pointed it out and Rita gasped. 'Are you kidding me?' She turned to her husband and pleaded, 'Saul, I can't do this, I'll fall, I'll...'

Saul calmed her down. 'It's all right, Rita. We'll cross together. It'll be fine, I promise.'

Aimee watched the sleeping magma bears. It seemed tip-toeing over their heads was their only means of escape.

CHAPTER 12

Maybe we should have stayed at the Station with Deputy Kevin and Carly, they both wondered. But it was too late now. Their plan was in motion.

Sophie and Tyler had managed to jump clear of the lorry before it turned in to the long flat expanse of the geysers. They now stood hidden behind some bushes as they watched the army set up their position. The large Mobile Command Unit had been parked up at a safe distance from the geyser itself. There was now a flurry of activity around it as troops came and went from the makeshift building.

A ground crew had then erected a tower and attached a winch to the top. Sophie watched as the nuclear bomb casing was driven over to the tower and then winched up and dangled before the geyser pointing downwards.

Did they just plan on dropping that thing in to the gap? The Army could be really stupid sometimes...

Tyler shifted nervously beside Sophie.

'Keep your eyes out for bears,' he offered, 'They could be all around us.'

Sophie hissed at him, 'Will you sit still? Just stick to the plan.'

'I'm just nervous.'

'Put it this way, at the moment it's the bears or a nuclear explosion. You're dying either way, Tyler.'

Tyler looked crushed. 'Aw, man. When you put it like that...'

Sophie cursed at how far away they were. They would need to cross an open expanse in front of a lot of guards. Perhaps they should have stayed on the transport a little longer.

If we'd have gotten any closer, we would have been spotted. At least from here, we can get the lay of the land, she thought.

She steadied her nerves. She was doing this for her Dad. She needed to remember that. Otherwise, this whole exercise was foolhardy.

'I didn't even get to say goodbye to my Mom...' Tyler muttered, having second thoughts. Sophie dismissed his comments.

'Have you ever gotten close to a bomb before?'

'My Dad was in Greenpeace,' Tyler said. 'I saw him take out a few bombs in his time. Those protests could get pretty intense.'

It was funny thinking how wild her friends lives had been. What had Sophie accomplished? A small town teenager, good grades, parents in law enforcement jobs. It's no wonder they thought she'd gone off the rails. But it was normal to rebel, to chase dreams and ideals – she just never imagined herself in a position like this.

It was oddly exhilarating.

'You think you can disarm it?' Sophie asked him.

'I've watched every tutorial on YouTube for everything ever,' Tyler snorted. 'I think I can take out a few wires on a detonator.'

Sophie wasn't convinced.

'The danger isn't the nuclear element, it's the timer. Once that thing sparks, there's no going back. Just got to take that out. It's not a problem.' Tyler hesitates. 'Hey, you got any WiFi? I could do with double checking my instructions...'

Sophie ignores him. 'I'll cause a distraction. You get close enough to the detonator.'

'I don't know, man. We're just, like... kids.'

Tyler was right. Who were they to save the park? But Sophie couldn't let self doubt stop them now. 'Tyler, if we don't try then everyone in this park gets wiped out. Do you want that?'

Tyler still looked unconvinced.

'Even the raccoons,' Sophie added.

A determination spread across his face. 'Let's do it for the raccoons,' he said, determinedly as he jumped out from behind cover and headed out across the valley.

All Sophie could think was, *Man, he must really like raccoons*.

The group held their collective breath as Brad stepped out on to the small ledge that ran around the edge of the broken tunnel floor. Below, the magma bears slept on silently beside a flowing river of boiling lava. Brad had thrown the equipment across the gap prior to stepping out.

He pressed his back against the rock, chin down staring in to the open space below him.

This was a bad idea.

One arm was outstretched, holding his oil lamp. It grew heavy in his outstretched arm and his muscles shook from holding it. The metal lamp clinked as he trembled – partly from exertion, partly from fear. He tried to hold himself together for the rest of the group, but on the inside he screamed.

'You're doing good, Brad.' The shout of encouragement came from Dennis. He steadied his breathing as he slowly shuffled along the cave wall.

'It's a little slippy.'

'Almost there.'

It felt like an eternity, but Brad was edging closer and closer to safety. With one final lunge, he staggered across and to safety. An audible sigh of relief went up from the rest of the party.

'Alright,' Brad sighed with relief, 'Who's next?'

The group looked to Rita, who shied away. 'I can't. I just can't.'

As Saul tried to settle her, Aimee stepped forward. 'I'll go.'

Brad nodded. He held up the lamp, giving Aimee as much light as he could. His arm still trembled. Aimee held Rita, looking her square in the eyes.

'Watch me,' she said, calmly.

Rita nodded, her whole body shaking.

Aimee took her time. She stepped out, legs stretched, arms clutching at the rock face behind her. She stared down at the fiery chasm below and froze. Brad saw her. He had done the same thing moments ago. 'Don't look down. Keep moving,' he instructed.

She closed her eyes, cleared her mind and then straightened her head, her neck stiff, staring straight ahead. Brad shouted in approval, but she could not hear him. She was now deep in concentration.

Shuffling quickly, Aimee took small steps along the ledge.

She heard a crack.

The stone gave way.

Aimee braced.

Rita screamed.

She did not move.

'Just a stone. You're all right,' shouted Brad. Her legs trembled and she struggled to move again. A few more small steps and her hand was in reach of Brad's. She grasped him tightly, knuckles white.

With a firm grip, Brad yanked at Aimee, pulling her clear of the chasm. She fell back away from the ledge. Safe.

'Rita, you're up.'

She tried to protest but Saul held her tight. 'We'll cross together,' he whispered. 'Don't worry. I won't let anything happen to you.'

Bravely, Saul stepped out on to the ledge. He offered his hand to Rita. She reached out, unable to control her shaking. She took her husband's hand and the fear subsided. Slowly, Saul pulled his wife towards him. Suddenly, Rita stepped out and was alongside him. He whispered more words of encouragement as they slowly moved across the ledge, Rita sobbing as she moved.

Brad took Saul's waist, steadying him on the other side. Sensing that her husband was no longer on the ledge with her, Rita panicked. She began to hyperventilate and froze on the spot.

'Just another step, Rita my love. One more step and you're home free.'

But Rita's eyes were starry, she was struggling to breathe. Aimee grew terrified, she thought Rita was about to pass out.

Saul remained calm. He leaned out to her, Brad anchoring him around the waist. With a panicked look in her eyes, Rita stepped towards her husband's arms blindly, ignoring her footing.

She slipped.

Aimee watched her drop.

Saul threw his arms tightly around his wife at the last split second. Brad threw himself backwards and Saul yanked his wife clear of the chasm. She tumbled in to Saul, landing on top of him in a heap on the floor.

They all caught their breath.

Saul grinned.

'Rita baby, I didn't know you still cared!'

Rita laughed, relieved to be clear of danger. For now.

Brad now watched as the last of the group, Dennis, stepped out. He was sure footed, reaching the middle of the ledge with ease. But Brad advised caution.

'Easy, Dennis. Take your time.'

Dennis smiled at his friend and took a moment.

Then, with misplaced confidence, Dennis tried to take a stride far too quickly.

He lost his balance, falling forward.

The group screamed in horror.

Dennis instinctively reached out to break his fall, grabbing for the mine cart track as he did so. But the one hundred year old track creaked and snapped under the unexpected weight. He span around as the track snapped and bent downwards.

Instinctively, Brad leapt to the edge of the chasm, reaching down desperate to save his friend.

Dennis' grip on the track was tight, but the track itself was now loose. He was slipping.

Brad reached a little further.

Managed to get a hold of Dennis' wrist – just in time as the track shook him loose. Dennis dangled over the deep chasm, grunting nervously.

Sweaty, Brad's hands were losing their grip on his friends' wrists.

'I've got you, buddy.'

'I can't hold on,' Dennis cried.

'I'll pull you up,' Brad shouted, but realistically he knew he didn't have a good enough grip. Brad watched his friend, who looked up in to his eyes desperately.

'I'm slipping. Brad, I'm...'

And Dennis slipped. His breath stopped in his throat. Brad's stomach turned as he saw his friend tumble backwards. He watched the horrified expression on Dennis' face as he fell back.

Rita screamed and turned away. In the second that it took him to fall, the rest watched wide eyed as Dennis headed straight for the lava.

His body crashed in to the molten rock, sending a ripple of magma out across the calm red fiery river.

A blood curdling shriek came from his burning body. His flesh burnt then crisped. His eyes melted from his sockets as he reached up towards his friend one last time before his charred arm turned to cinder.

Beside his charring corpse, a magma bear opened its eyes and sniffed at the air.

Meat.

It growled and its comrades stirred.

Brad gasped. 'Fuck.'

Slowly, hundreds of magma bears rose from their slumber and their gaze turned upward to the commotion coming from the tunnel above.

And they were angry.

Scrambling to his feet, Brad gathered the supplies.

'Run,' he said.

But nobody moved.

Dennis was dead. Burnt to death before their eyes.

'Run.'

But they were frozen to the spot. Trapped in a tunnel with hundreds of hungry magma bears.

Brad's eyes were wild. He roared louder than any magma bear.

'*RUN!*'

CHAPTER 13

An Army Jeep brought Agent Daniels to the site of the geyser. He stepped from the vehicle and surveyed the landscape. The National Guard were in the final stages of preparation. The bomb was teetering over the geyser with a small specially constructed ledge giving his men access for programming the timer.

A perimeter had been established along the valley. Several gun turrets and groups of soldiers watched for any intruders. There were no bears. All in all a successful operation. He took some binoculars from a passing soldier and smiled as he looked out over the horizon.

'I love the smell of barbecued bear in the morning,' he smiled.

'Looking for someone?' a young voice asked beside him. He turned to find Sophie stood there. She crossed her arms defiantly.'It best be my Dad. Because if you blow this park up with him inside, I'm gonna be super pissed.'

Agent Daniels could not suppress a grin. He patted Sophie on the head, patronisingly. 'Who's your Daddy, little girl?' he asked.

'Sheriff Walker.'

She looked around to see if Tyler had managed to break away. He was nowhere to be seen. Still, she hoped that wandering on to the site was about to cause enough distraction for them to concentrate on her and not on any friends she may have brought along.

'I'm so sorry, angel,' Daniels offered, mockingly, 'Your Daddy has gone to heaven with the rest of the park. Now if you'll run along like a good girl, I'm pretty busy right now.' He turned back to his binoculars, uninterested.

Not satisfied with her distraction, Sophie tried to goad Daniels further. 'You government types are all the same,' she laughs dismissively, 'Big ego's to make up for where you're lacking elsewhere. One of those bears shows up here, you'll beg for your life just like everyone else.'

Daniels quickly turned back to Sophie, grabbing her around the neck. 'You think you're so brave, don't you?' He whispered in her ear as she struggled for breath. 'You're from a generation that thinks you can say and do anything you like and there'll be no consequences. Well, I've got news for you, sweetheart. This is a new America. People won't stand by and listen to that hippy bullshit any more. We make a stand. And if that means blowing a fucking hole through your pretty little head, then so be it.'

He relaxed his grip. Sophie struggled free.

'And for the record, I'm not your typical *government type*. I'm Environmental fucking Protection. And this is how I save the world. Fun, isn't it?' Daniels casually turned away, shouting to a nearby Guard. 'Can you get this teenager out of my camp, please? How did she get in here anyway?'

Before he could respond, another Guard approached with Tyler held by the collar. Sophie's heart immediately sank.

'Looks like she had a friend, sir.' The Guard threw Tyler to the floor. Sophie rushed to him and checked he was okay. His left eye was swollen. She tried to cradle his head, but he winced in pain.

'I'm sorry, Sophie.'

'It's okay, Tyler. You tried.'

'He wasn't in Greenpeace,' Tyler stammered.

'What?' Sophie didn't understand.

'All that stuff I've said. The protests, the time I saved the whales with my Dad, the hunger strike at the nuclear plant.' Tyler paused. 'My Dad is an accountant. I just thought... you wouldn't like me, or something...'

Sophie was speechless.

Daniels wasn't. 'They're breaking my heart, over here. Take them away before love conquers the day. I can feel my heart growing two sizes as it is.'

The Guard continued, 'He was trying to get close to the bomb.'

'Was he, now.' Daniels crouched before the fallen Tyler. 'Didn't your parents teach you not to play with explosives? What did you hope to accomplish? Hmm?' Tyler said nothing. Agent Daniels prodded at his swollen and bruised face. Tyler screamed. 'What did you hope to achieve?'

'Stop it! Leave him alone!'

Daniels had had enough. No matter how hard he tried, nobody in this park seemed to understand that what they were doing was in everybody's interests. And if they couldn't accept that, he may as well be the bad guy.

He sighed, 'Put them in my car. I'll take them back to the Station.'

'Are you not sticking around for the detonation, sir?' the Guard asked.

Army types. They sure liked it when things went boom.

'I wouldn't want to crowd out your fun, soldier. I'll let you proceed as planned.'

'You can't!' Sophie protested, 'I won't let you blow the geyser up!'

Daniels ignored her. He continued, 'Has the timer been set?'

'Armed and activated, sir.'

Daniels gave Sophie a shrug and a smirk. 'Looks like I can and I will. Shall we head back?' He indicated towards his Jeep. Hesitantly, Sophie helped Tyler to his feet. He staggered slowly towards the vehicle using Sophie as a support. Agent Daniels followed right behind.

On the far perimeter, there was suddenly a buzz of activity. Sophie heard scattered pops of gunfire. The Guard reached for his radio and spoke to his men. Agent Daniels was distracted.

The gunfire became more prolonged, Sophie could hear shouting.

Daniels called the Guard back. 'What's going on?'

'Bears spotted at the perimeter, sir.'

Sophie watched as Guards came streaming past them heading towards the action, each carrying a rifle. She thought of all those hunters back at the Ranger Station. All their weapons and it didn't help against what happened. The National Guard didn't stand a chance.

'Contain them,' Daniels ordered, suddenly all business again. He looked at Sophie and Tyler, his face now blank. No smugness. No smirk. 'You two, with me.'

There was a scream.

In the distance, a bear had jumped on one of the gun turrets and was tearing the soldier apart. The bear was huge. Sophie realised just how dangerous it was to be out in the open. Could one of these had got her Dad? He wouldn't have stood a chance.

More bears lunged out from the trees, forcing the Army further back. The few pockets of men who stood their ground were dismantled with ease. A swift claw across the chest and a soldiers insides spilled across the valley floor. A well placed foot with the right amount of pressure and a soldier's skull burst from his scalp.

It was a massacre.

Sophie looked for an exit point, but it was no use. The camp was surrounded. The magma bears were unstoppable.

A bear came running towards them at full speed. Agent Daniels yelped, grabbing the Guard and throwing him between himself and the bear.

It accepted the gift of flesh willingly, crunching on the fallen Guard as Daniels sprinted towards his Jeep. Sophie watched him go. 'Come on, we need to keep up.'

'I can't Sophie. I don't think I can walk. Just leave me.' Tyler crumpled to the floor.

'I'll get help. I'll bring the Jeep around.'

Tyler nodded. Sophie raced off towards Agent Daniels.

He reached the Jeep, clambering in to the drivers side. The ignition fired. He looked to Sophie.

'Wait up! He needs help!' Sophie shouted, pointing to Tyler.

Daniels gave her the finger.

Sophie realised she was alone.

She turned back to Tyler, scooped him up off the floor and together they limped away as fast as they could towards cover.

Agent Daniels put his foot on the gas, but the Jeep struggled to move. 'Come on...' he growled. The engine roared, but the Jeep stayed put. 'COME ON!' he shouted, frustrated.

Something must be weighing it down.

Must weigh a ton...

He looked in the rearview mirror.

A magma bear growled at him from the back seat.

Screaming, he prised the door open, leapt from the Jeep and ran.

A group of soldiers had one bear contained. The bear stood growling as the soldiers surrounded it and fired an endless stream of bullets. The bear staggered, pieces of its rocky coat chipping away and large cuts of magma flowing from under his skin. The soldiers moved in, the bear contained. They tightened the circle, moving ever closer and closer.

Sophie tried to run, Tyler limping against her shoulder. She saw the soldiers now standing above the fallen bear – from where she stood, it looked as though they were shooting point blank in its face.

The bear grunted, somewhat resigned. Then suddenly, it lunged forward, its massive jaws closing down on a soldiers torso.

He didn't let go. Instead, he swung the soldiers' limp body from side to side, knocking his squad mates down like pins.

Then, he playfully tossed the limp body in to the air and tore at it as it came down. The soldiers' skin flayed, his exposed muscles singed and his sharp white broken bones crashed to the floor in a mangled heap. Before the rest could regroup, another two bears descended to pick up the scraps. They stood over their prey and they fed.

Sophie sped on. Towards the trees. Towards shelter.

A figure screamed past them.

It was Agent Daniels.

He almost bowled them over as he fled, diving in to the undergrowth. Sophie gritted her teeth. 'Bastard,' she muttered. This was all Daniels' doing. How many had died? How many more were about to die?

She caught something in the corner of her eye. An approaching bear.

It bounded towards them.

How could she have been so careless? She was distracted by Daniels and now it could cost them their lives...

Quickly, she threw herself to the ground – dragging Tyler down with her. They held each other tight.

The bear pounced.

Right over them.

In to an approaching group of soldiers. They all went down, shrieking in pain as it tore at them.

Sophie grabbed Tyler by the collar, 'Go.'

They crawled, staying as low as they could, towards the trees. Another bear charged, its paws narrowly missing Sophie's head as it ran in to the fray. Reaching the undergrowth, they roll in to the long grass and hold their breath.

Meanwhile, Agent Daniels continued to sprint. The battlefield was a distant echo as he leapt over roots and ducked vines in his attempt to escape. A large tree root lay ahead and Daniels charged on, hurdling over the large obstacle.

As his right foot landed, he heard a snap.

He continued, bounding on to his left foot, then brought his right to bear.

It was no longer there.

The bloody stump hit the ground and he screamed in pain. He tumbled forward, rolling to a halt.

A warm feeling spread up his knee and to his waist. When he glanced down, he could see his foot had been taken off at the calf. A clean cut. The pain was unbearable.

He looked to where he had fell. There was a large bear trap on the floor. Its metallic jaws had snapped shut and a small bloodied limb lay underneath.

He was suddenly cold. His skin immediately clammy.

Agent Daniels closed his eyes...

...When next they opened, he heard the sound of chewing. He smiled, a distant memory of his parents old barbecues springing to mind for no reason. His mouth almost watered, imagining a big juicy hamburger, covered in 'slaw.

He tried to sit up.

He couldn't.

Suddenly lucid, he glanced down to find the source of the chomping sound. A magma bear stood over him, casually stripping the meat from his legs.

Agent Daniels screamed so loud that he tore his vocal chords. And then the bear ripped out his throat.

Deputy Kevin walked silently in to the meeting room. The Mayor was sat staring at the map. A large army issue radio was sat next to him. Neither man spoke. Silently, Kevin reached for the radio and turned the sound on.

There were loud bursts of gunfire, the occasional yelp from men as they were slaughtered...

The Mayor slammed his fist on to the table.

'Goddamnit, will you turn that shit off?'

'They sound in a bad way,' Kevin stated. The Mayor just grunted. Kevin sat beside him, feeling helpless. Sophie and Tyler had gone to prevent a detonation and were now likely dead in the ensuing battle. Hank and Lori had disappeared, the park's visitors were slaughtered and the rest of the Park Rangers were lost.

He resented being sat there with the Mayor and with Carly. If he told her how badly things were going at the geyser, she would be inconsolable. Her friends had gone to their deaths.

The Mayor sighed, 'The Army can't stop this. We've got a nuclear weapon sat in the park surrounded by giant killer *dino-bears*, or something. Face it son, this is how it ends.'

'Hank will fix this.'

'Hank is dead.'

Deputy Kevin didn't believe that. Hank was a tough, cantankerous old bastard. He was out there, somewhere. He had to be.

Carly appeared at the door. 'Deputy, will you come look at this.'

Kevin sat deep in thought. He didn't hear.

'Deputy.'

'Not now, Carly. I need to think,' he said without looking up. The last thing he needed was another teenage plan. More blood on his hands.

Sophie... Why did I let you go?

'Seriously, Deputy. You need to come here. Now.'

Kevin's ears pricked up. His stomach turned with dread. Carly's tone did not fill him with confidence. He strode out of the meeting room and across reception. Carly pointed him towards a window.

He looked out.

Nothing.

'Looks pretty quiet.' *As you might expect*, he thought. *No one left.*

'In the trees,' she indicated.

Kevin squinted towards the trees. The sun was slowly sinking, the large trees now cast long dark shadows towards the Ranger Station. But in the darkness, something was watching.

He could see two red orbs.

Not orbs. Eyes. Glowing red eyes.

And the more he looked, the more he saw. He tried to count them. Ten. Twenty. At least forty pairs of eyes, watching and waiting from the forest.

'We're in big trouble,' he muttered.

The Mayor emerged from the meeting room. 'Tell me something I don't know.'

'Okay,' Kevin chose his words carefully. 'You're about to get to see some of those *dino-bears* up close...'

Slowly, the shadows started to advance.

From the tall grass, Sophie watched as the base was decimated. Bears lapped from puddles of blood that had formed on the ground. The few scatterings of soldiers that remain were now running for their lives and being brought down with a massive claw to the back.

She watched as a bear caught his long claws in a soldier, who was struggling to break free. He tried to sprint, but the bear yanked him back with one claw. There was a snap and his spine was ripped from his back. The body crumpled to the floor. The bear didn't even feast. It just nonchalantly walked away from the corpse, looking for its next kill. Sophie stifled her cries. Tyler couldn't look.

One particular man then ran across the battlefield and Sophie recognised him as the Sergeant back at the Ranger Station. He had large semi automatics in each hand and shouted noisily as he swung around, his bullets firing in a wide arch.

A bear crept up behind him. He turned and froze.

It rose on its hind feet, looming over him.

Then swatted at him, a huge paw thwacking him in the side of the head. The force was enough to tear his head from his body and it sailed through the air and bounced along the floor, landing at the feet of another magma bear who swallowed it whole.

The headless body of the Sergeant fell to the floor, blood still pumping fron between his shoulders. The bear quenched its thirst, drinking from his neck like it was a water fountain.

Sophie held back her vomit.

The Army was now thin in numbers and it occurred to her that once the bears had finished feasting, they would be on the look out for more victims.

'We need to move further away,' she whispered to the bruised Tyler. 'Do you think you can move?'

He nodded, 'I'm okay. I can't see too well, though.' His swollen eye was a mess. A result of the beating given to him for trespassing on this site. Sophie silently hoped Agent Daniels had run in to an entire den of the bears.

Sophie helped Tyler to his feet. He straightened up.

He looked past Sophie, eyes wide.

She felt the sunlight fade as a shadow fell over her.

Turning, Sophie found a huge magma bear stood before them. Its eyes burnt with rage and hunger.

Then she heard a voice from behind her. A voice she hadn't heard since this all started. What had he called her back at the Ranger Station?

The voice said; 'Hey, girly. Miss me?'

Sophie stood between the magma bear and Ed.

He was covered in mud, his shirt torn from his chest, the remnants of an army vest thrown over him – she wondered if it was his or he had taken it from a nearby body.

Ed reached in to a pocket and pulled out a grenade. He tore the pin out with his teeth. With the pin still in his teeth, he grinned, 'The National Park Association kindly reminds y'all not to feed the bears.'

And with that, he threw the grenade at the bear, who instinctively caught it in his mouth and swallowed.

The bear paused.

Then it exploded.

Sophie and Tyler shielded their eyes. The splash of blood burnt their skin. They winced as they came out in blisters.

But they were alive.

Ed winked, 'We thank you for your cooperation.'

Moving quickly, Ed grabbed a huge piece of the bears rib cage and ushered the teenagers underneath it. He pulled it closed around them and they sat, waiting for the slaughter to finish.

CHAPTER 14

They had been walking for an hour without incident, now. It was warm enough to dry their clothes out from their encounter with the waterfall. Most of the journey was silent. Lori could sense both Avon and Hank were keeping their ears open for any signs of pursuit. They had both chastised themselves for getting suckered by those magma bears at the bridge – neither man had any intention of it happening again.

As it happened, diving from the bridge had cut about half an hour from their journey. Once they had crossed the waterfall, they needed to descend in to the valley below. Avon had joked that they had taken the 'shortcut'.

Down here, the forest was much more dense. Mostly, the trees were overgrown and unkempt – which cut out a lot of the sunlight and increased the humidity. Occasionally, they stepped in to unfiltered sunlight and basked in its warming glow, however brief.

Lori noticed that for the past mile or so they had been following a rock wall. No doubt this was part of the cliff face that ran up to the waterfall. There was something strangely comforting about having the wall to one side – if they were going to be ambushed, at least it could only come from one direction.

Eventually, the rock face turned away and they followed it around a corner. Lori noticed that the consistency of the rock was changing too. This looked shaped, chiselled. Like people had begun to carve in to this rock a very long time ago.

When they cleared the next row of trees, Lori's suspicion was confirmed.

A man made grove stood before them, leading to a large imposing rock doorway carved in to the rock. It was like something out of an *Indiana Jones* movie.

Either side of the open doorway stood two giant totems, carved from the trees that had been cleared. They were awe inspiring. Lori couldn't help but feel she had seen these somewhere before and she realised that Avon's totem back at the cabin was a small scale replica of these.

And far more amateur. Had Avon carved it himself? She wondered how much time Avon had spent here on his own in quiet contemplation. It must have been bliss.

She caught a look of admiration on Hank's face as he stood staring at the entrance to the Temple. His jaw was wide open. Lori was fascinated that Hank had never been here before.

Avon stopped beside his friend and placed a welcoming hand on to his shoulder. 'Beautiful, isn't it?'

Hank was speechless. Avon smiled at Lori, who shook her head in disbelief.

'Did your family carve them?' she asked.

'So I'm told.' Avon pointed out some of the

features, running his hand lovingly across the woodwork, 'The finer detail was carved using bear claws and teeth. As I said, no piece from the hunt left to waste.'

For totems as detailed as this to have been carved from claws and teeth Lori considered the work to be a masterpiece. Instantly she had a pang of regret that so many people hadn't seen this. Had she known, she would have come here every day.

'Who else knows about this place?'

Avon shrugged, 'Oh, it's on the tourist trail, but it's far enough off the beaten track that it's largely forgotten. If they come by this way, it's to see the Falls, not the weird Bear Temple.'

All it had taken was an earth shattering quake and some ancient killer bears to bring them here, she chastised herself. Lori hoped Avon was right. This was a massive leap of faith to make while the rest of the park was in tatters. She could sense that Hank was thinking it as he sat quietly on a rock in silent contemplation.

She knew how tough it was for the old Sheriff, how derisory he had been back at the cabin – now stood in front of the Bear Temple preparing some ceremony to send the monster bears back where they came from. She could hardly believe it herself, and she wasn't having to contend with the loss of contact with a teenage daughter.

Avon spoke quietly to Lori. 'I'll go see to the preparations,' and indicated in the direction of Hank. She nodded. Avon went in to the Temple, leaving Lori and Hank alone.

After a few moments, Lori quietly approached and sat alongside Hank. He seemed to appreciate the company.

Slowly, he took his cell phone from his pocket and checked it. There was still no signal and his battery was now low. Out of support, Lori checked hers. Nothing.

Hank reflected for a few moments.

'I still can't get any signal,' he said, gravely.

Lori tried to keep her tone light. She smiled, 'The curse of technology. We all hate relying on it, but we miss it when it doesn't work.'

Hank stared ahead, not speaking. His thoughts clearly elsewhere. Lori chose to let him reflect. It was better to have his mind wander now than later when he may need his wits to get back safely.

'I just can't stop thinking about her.' His voice was soft, more tender than Lori had ever known. Lori's heart broke for him.

'You saw her, Hank,' she tried to reassure him. 'She's a natural leader. She's strong, like her Dad.' Hank couldn't help but smile, a small burst of pride hearing Lori compare the two of them. She added, 'You think she's gonna let some mutant bears slow her down?'

Hank laughed this time. Lori had stifle a hysterical giggle herself. How many times in her life would she get to say that?

'You know how ridiculous that sounds?' Hank chuckled.

Lori nudged her elbow against his ribs playfully. 'No more ridiculous than Hank Walker on a spiritual quest to communicate with the All Mother.'

Hank guffawed. Lori was right. As ridiculous as this situation was, Hank had found himself in an even weirder place. 'How about that,' he said. 'Just do me a favour and don't tell anyone that I came on this crazy ride. I'm a respected man, I need to maintain some credibility. Praying to the Bear God is something I'd never live down.'

Lori nodded in agreement, 'That makes two of us, Sheriff. I promise never to speak of this again.' She crossed her heart, mockingly and Hank did the same.

A few more minutes passed between them. Avon was nowhere to be seen. Lori glanced back at the Temple. The glow of lit torches could be seen coming from within and the occasional mutter as Avon studied his books.

Hank reached for a flask of water and took a large gulp before handing it to Lori. She took a sip and slowly replaced the cap. As she passed it back to Hank, she caught his eye and said, 'Thank you for coming.'

Hank looked at her, confused.

She continued, 'I wouldn't have blamed you if you'd stayed at the cabin. Or if you'd tried to fight your way back down to the geyser.' She paused, considering her next few words. 'I don't want to pretend like I know what your motivation was, whether you're just trying to keep yourself busy or whether you truly want to believe Avon can make a difference here, but I'm glad you came along.'

Hank nodded in silent agreement.

'My Dad was a Pastor,' Hank sighed, 'Brought us up to follow the Bible without question. We listened as he practised his sermons, we studied the Bible, we went to Church every Sunday.' Hank shot a glance to the large totems stood at the Temple entrance. 'We believed without question, because my father told me that faith was the most important thing in the world.'

Lori sensed that Hank had disagreed with his

father. She said nothing, waiting for him to continue willingly.

'When he died, I just didn't know what to believe. I was angry. I didn't understand how a man who had devoted his life to religion could go through such pain.' Hank was fighting back angry tears. 'What had it all been for?'

He took a few moments, taking the flask and another gulp of water. After a few deep breaths, he went on; 'I gave up my faith, decided that if I couldn't see it here and now in front of me, then I shouldn't waste my time on it.'

And there it was. The bears were real. They had chased them to this Temple. Even Hank couldn't deny Avon's stories any more.

Hank sighed, 'I guess I've been wanting something to believe in ever since.'

There was a look on Hank's face, like a burden had finally been lifted. That he had finally put this in to words in a place that he had sworn never to speak of again – Lori realised this was almost a confessional. Perhaps Hank didn't expect to make it back alive, maybe he just had to tell someone while he still could. Or maybe he truly trusted Lori.

Either way, she felt closer to the Sheriff than she ever had been. She placed a supportive hand upon his arm and he looked up. 'This day's been full of surprises so far, Sheriff. Why let it end here?'

Hank nodded knowingly and Lori stood up to stretch. She paced to the Temple entrance, then stopped.

There was something watching.

Hank hadn't noticed. She whispered to him.

His head shot up, suddenly alert. Lori beckoned to him and slowly, without drawing attention, he crossed to her position.

Lori was frozen still, staring at the edge of the forest. Hank joined her and followed her gaze.

She had spotted a bear.

It stood calmly, watching.

Waiting.

'Another,' she whispered, nervously. Her legs shook. She wanted to run. She flinched, but Hank caught her arm. He wasn't moving.

Hank didn't even look afraid.

'No,' he whispered to her calmly, 'It's not one of them.'

She looked harder – the bear that watched them was small in comparison. Its fur was ragged, but most definitely hair. His eyes were a dark brown. The snout of the bear sniffed at them as he watched from a distance.

Lori realised who this was.

'Is that Avon's...'

'...Avon's Guide, yes,' Hank finished. Lori noted that Hank had referred to it as a *Guide* and not a *Pet*. Perhaps there truly was hope for the Sheriff after all.

She struggled to remember its name. Hank helped, 'It's Spirit. He must have followed us here.'

Lori watched. 'Are we supposed to...' she struggled with her question, 'Are we supposed to invite it in, or something?' She waited awkwardly. The bear just watched them, quite happily.

'Maybe we should let it make its own mind up,' Hank suggested.

With their eyes locked on Spirit, Hank and Lori backed in to the Temple and looked for Avon.

Brad felt like he had been running for hours. His legs ached, his chest was tight. He wondered how bad Saul and Rita must have felt, but the group was now in full fight or flight mode. For the first few minutes, they could hear the magma bears thudding down the tunnel, their claws scraping at the rock, their breathing heavy.

He wondered how well they could adapt to darkness. Would these tunnels pose as much of a challenge to a magma bear as it did to a human? Maybe that's why they slept.

Eventually, they reached a junction. Several tunnels intersected, the mine cart tracks split in multiple directions with a single lever in the centre to control the lines.

The stamina of the group began to waver. Aimee was doubled over beside the wall, coughing up bile. Saul was clutching at his chest, heart racing. Rita's lungs were rasping, desperately trying to grab what oxygen they could.

Brad listened.

He couldn't hear the bears. Maybe they had lost them...

He crumpled to the floor, taking a moment to breathe himself. Aimee staggered over and threw herself down beside him. 'We can't stay here,' she gasped.

'I think we've lost them,' Brad replied. 'Take a few minutes, rest up. One last push, that's all we need.'

Rita helped Saul to a rock and sat him down. She was still weeping.

Aimee grabbed the map from Brad and they began to check their route.

Saul muttered, 'They can't be far behind us. They'll never stop. You saw the size of them, the number of them. We need to keep moving.'

'In a minute. Take a breath,' Brad growled.

They all sat for a few minutes. Rita dabbed at her eyes with a sleeve. She couldn't control the tears any longer. 'Poor Dennis. His screams...' she cried. Saul shushed her as he held her head.

'Rita, dear, we have to stay focused on getting out of here,' he told her, 'You dwell on what you've seen and snap, you're done for. You understand?' But Rita was inconsolable. Saul changed tact, he needed to keep his wife focused on escape. Calmly, he told her; 'Think of the kids, Rita. Think of our grandchildren. Will you do that for me?'

It seemed to work. Rita started to compose herself, calming her breathing. After a few moments, she started to relax. 'I'm sorry, Saul. I'm just so scared. Those bears, they're so...'

Saul interrupted her, preventing another outburst. 'I know. But we've got to fight.' He held her tight. Saul didn't expect he would see his family again, but he couldn't tell his wife that. Instead, he reminisced, 'Remember when David was sick?'

Rita perked up, the memory of her son as an infant bringing a momentary reprieve. 'You always were so protective over that son of ours.'

'I used to sit by his crib all night, remember?' Saul prompted.

His wife laughed, 'And doze off in to your breakfast cereal. How you managed to hold down a job, I'll never know.' She shook her head.

Saul shrugged. 'I was a new father. I worried.'

'But you never stopped to enjoy it,' Rita remembered chastising him about it at the time. 'Your first son.'

'You remember what you said to me?' he asked.

She nodded, 'I told you to let me do the worrying for both us.'

He squeezed her tight. 'And I had the best night's sleep I'd ever had.'

Rita burst out laughing. She remembered the night all too well. 'You snored so loud. I never caught a wink.'

'But now I'm asking you. Rita, let me do the worrying for both us.' He didn't want this to sound like his final words to her, but he had to let her know. Whatever happened next. 'You'll get out of here. You'll go back home to our beautiful grandchildren and you'll forget all about what happened here.'

Rita tried to avoid his gaze, but Saul looked her deep in the eyes, 'Hey, I promise,' he said. And Rita smiled, reassured.

She placed her head on his chest and Saul stared in to the darkness, contemplating his next steps.

Aimee continued to study the map. Brad leaned across and checked it with her. She ran her finger along the line, turning the map slightly to check it against their current position.

'We good?' Brad asked.

'I just need to double check,' Aimee muttered. She caught brad's gaze. His face was stony, his eyes disguising his pain. She tried to speak to him; 'Look, what happened back there...'

But Brad just cut her off. 'I don't want to talk about it. We've all lost good people today,' he said, matter-of-fact, and Aimee felt another well of sadness for Nick. 'Let's make sure it's not for nothing, eh?' Brad encouraged.

Aimee nodded, then indicated to the tunnel that branched off to the right.

'This way. Not far now.'

'Good.' Brad stood up and surveyed his party. They all looked to him for guidance. He had lost Ed and Dennis, but he couldn't think about that now. He had to think about survival. 'Let's move out.'

They all rose. Rita joined Aimee and the two of them started towards the tunnel. As Brad moved away, Saul caught him by the arm and held him back. 'Hold up.' Saul's tone was conspiratorial. Brad waited.

'We've found their den. Are we really just going to run away?' Saul asked, bitterly.

The thought had crossed Brad's mind, but how many more had to die? Going back was suicide.

'You have a better idea?' he asked Saul.

'Well, we should at least stop them from following us, but if there's any way to seal these tunnels up, I think we should take it.'

Brad considered this for a few moments before shaking his head. 'It's too risky.'

Saul was adamant, 'Risky is walking away and leaving those bears to roam free. We need to block them in, send them to sleep permanently.'

He knew Saul was right. He gave it some thought, then took Dennis' rucksack from his shoulder cautiously. He checked that Aimee and Rita were out of sight, then unzipped the bag and showed Saul the contents.

'Dynamite?'

'We found it in the first tunnel.'

Saul was enthused. He clapped a hand on brad's shoulder, enthusiastically. 'Perfect, we can just blow them all back to Hell.'

'It's not that simple,' Brad kept his voice low, 'We didn't find any detonators. We can't charge these things remotely.'

There was a pause as Saul realised what Brad was getting at. If they wanted to detonate, they needed to do so manually. Light the short fuse and say your prayers. Saul hesitated.

Brad said, 'I'll have to stay behind.'

Saul started to object, but Brad waved him off. 'No arguing. Let's just get this job done, okay? Before those things track us down.' He hoped that he would be the last to die. He might even save the whole park. 'I'll find a cart, load it with what we have, drive it back down towards their den...'

'Let me help you get started,' came a voice from the tunnel. It was Aimee. She had come back and happened upon the conversation. She got close to Brad, 'Just make sure you take out all of those fuckers.'

Brad nodded.

Saul ushered Aimee away. 'Actually, you stay with Rita. I'll give Brad a hand.' Aimee tried to object, but Saul gave her a pleading look. She suspected his motives, but she backed away.

Aimee returned to Rita as Saul and Brad disappeared up a tunnel, conspiratorially.

The scrape of a giant claw against the wooden walls of the Ranger Station made Kevin's hair stand on end. The wooden floorboards of the porch creaked and snapped as the monsters advanced.

The Ranger Station was surrounded.

The door banged, Kevin stepped back. He checked on Carly – she was hiding under the reception desk. The Mayor stood in the middle of the room clutching an axe.

'What do we do?' Carly cried.

'It'll hold,' Kevin said. It was supposed to be reassuring, but it was clear that the structure of the building was no match for bears of this size.

Another bang at the door. The frame shuddered.

A wooden door panel splintered.

Something tried to prise its way past the panel. Kevin realised that it was a snout. The panel fell away and the bears face was fully visible in the small gap. Its nostrils flared, its teeth gnashed.

Carly screamed.

It only seemed to drive the bear on.

Kevin rushed for Hank's office. He rifled through a drawer, looking for a weapon.

Found it.

Hank's old service revolver. Kevin didn't even know how to use it. Was it loaded? Who'd keep a loaded gun in a drawer? He felt around for any loose bullets, but suddenly.

Crash!

A paw came smashing through the window, grabbing for him. He dived out of the way at the last second. The outstretched claw was long enough to reach the desk. It swiped at it, cutting the desk clean in two and Kevin realised just how big these mutant bears actually were.

He ran from the office, slamming the door shut behind him.

'Stay away from the windows!'

One by one, the surrounding windows smashed, exploratory paws groping their way in. The bear at the door continued to push at the gap in the panel. The door frame splintered and strained.

'You have to save me,' the Mayor cried, but he was far from Kevin's thoughts at that moment.

He needed an escape plan.

The door frame burst.

The bear pushed his head through as wood exploded across the room. He let out a triumphant roar and the rest acknowledged his success. The bears shoulders were still too large to squeeze in to the room.

They had a limited amount of time.

Kevin looked up.

The skylight.

Where was the ladder?

He crossed to the supply cupboard and started pulling out the accumulated junk.

The ladder was at the back of the cupboard.

Another frame splintered, this time a window. A bear had its head through the gap, teeth bare, slobber spraying the room. Kevin placed the ladder in the centre of the room, trying to control his trembling hands.

'I'll make sure it's clear, then follow me up,' he told Carly.

Quickly, he climbed the ladder and pushed open the skylight. He took a cautious look out across the roof, revolver at the ready.

Clear.

'Okay, let's go,' he shouted down. The bear at the door was almost free, his reach so close...

Carly climbed two steps of the ladder before she was stopped.

The Mayor grabbed her and threw her to one side. She staggered backwards, almost within reach of the bear.

'What are you doing?' she cried.

'Age before beauty,' he retorted.

Kevin was enraged. 'Get out of the way! She'll be killed!'

'Better her than me,' he snarled as he started to climb.

Kevin felt a wave of anger. His hands shook. He reached down, revolver in hand, and clubbed the Mayor across the face with the butt of the gun.

He fell backward, nose busted.

Carly wasted no time in climbing up. Kevin just looked down at the Mayor, the two men locking eyes. 'I'm sorry,' Kevin said.

The Mayor let out a blood curdling scream as the bear burst free from the door and slashed at him. Kevin turned away, closing the skylight behind him.

Now there were two.

Hank and Lori followed the torchlight down a corridor, which opened in to a large inner chamber. The rock walls were cool to the touch, with large torches fastened at equal distance. Between each torch was carved a large portrait of a bear, or various scenes from old folk tales. Hank stood looking at them, deciphering each one.

Lori however was drawn to the centre of the room. To the sound of a large drum, played by Avon. He stood on a raised dais, a stone pillar marking each corner. To Lori, it looked like an altar – perhaps where a sacrifice may have been made.

Avon stood in the centre, banging the drum, eyes closed, chanting in an ancient dialect.

Lori gave Hank a nudge, 'I guess he started without us.'

But Hank was still looking around the room in awe. Lori was surprised, 'You've really not been here before, have you?'

Hank gave no excuses. 'I didn't think it would be this big.'

'Seriously?' How long have you been a Ranger?'

'I just never thought it was anything special,' Hank admitted. But it was clear from the look on his face that he now thought quite differently. 'Turns out I was wrong,' he said, 'very wrong.'

Suddenly, Avon ceased his chant and his eyes opened wide. He held out his hands – it was as if he couldn't see Lori and Hank stood there. He was completely in the moment.

He began to recite a prayer.

'All Mother, bringer of life, of sustenance, of warmth, of shelter;

I see your World and I give thanks for your abundance.

I stand before you, in awe of your power and I tremble at your magnificence,

I have felt your wrath and I stand awaiting judgement.'

Lori felt a faint tremor. She looked to Hank. His face said that he felt it too. They waited nervously, the tremor becoming more and more pronounced. Then they felt it. The walls shook – not violently, just gradually – and the dust was unsettled from corners and fell from the pillars.

Lori watched, anxiously.

Then there was another sound. Not a tremor, but a grunt.

A sniff.

A snort.

Hank braced himself. 'That doesn't sound good,' he said. Avon didn't notice him. He just continued to pray.

'Spirit?' Lori hoped. Perhaps Avon's Guide had decided to come in after all?

'Let's hope so,' Hank echoed.

Avon carried on;

'I call you before me, Great Mother of Life;

That we may gaze upon you and pray your forgiveness.

Show us mercy, All Mother.'

And with that, Avon returned to his chanting. Lori became aware of a shuffling in a darkened passageway. It was not the direction from which they entered. Somewhere that led deeper in to the cave.

There was a shape in the darkness. Lori and Hank both watched, unable to tear their eyes away.

Slowly, the figure emerged. A great hulking bear. It was hard for Lori to make out its features – was this a grizzly? Or a magma bear?

As if to answer, its eyes began to blaze with fire and she became acutely aware of that smell of sulphur that accompanied these monsters. It crept from the shadows, watching them both.

As it entered the glow of the chamber, its rocky skin bristled in anger and it let out a growl of warning.

Lori wanted to back away, to run as far as she could, but Hank held her arm. They needed to stay.

'Let's hope the All Mother is in a forgiving mood,' Hank said.

Together, they stood huddled, watching helplessly as the bear crept across the sanctum. All the while Avon remained standing, his eyes closed, arms outstretched.

Completely vulnerable.

CHAPTER 15

The Mobile Command Unit was abandoned.

It stood deserted amongst the scattered bodies next to the geyser. The soldiers were decimated, the equipment trampled and trails of blood running across the encampment. A number of bears sat engorged and contented, chewing on the bones of their prey without a care.

All blissfully unaware of the nuclear bomb casing that still dangled precariously from a tower next to the geyser.

The timer continued to count down.

In the corner of the battlefield, there was a hint of movement. A large bear carcass – the only one in sight – began to shift. The exposed ribcage teetered and then overturned.

Ed staggered out from underneath it, wiping his tattered vest clean. He was scarred, his skin covered in minor burns.

Behind him, Sophie and Tyler emerged, gasping.

'Ew, gross,' Sophie winced. She would never eat ribs again.

Tyler grimaced, 'I think I got some in my mouth.'

Ed watched Sophie as she climbed to her feet. He wore a ridiculous grin that reminded Sophie of their altercation early that morning.

'I saw you this morning. I think I smashed your tail light,' Sophie rambled, apologetically. She didn't have to like him to know he'd saved their lives. 'You're alive,' she said.

'How 'bout that,' Ed smirked.

'I guess we should thank you.'

Ed looked out across the geyser. 'Don't thank me just yet, babydoll. Plenty more of 'em critters to get through 'fore we home safe.' He tried to assess the situation.

'Where's the rest of your guys?' Sophie asked, then immediately regretted it.

Ed was silent.

'I'm sorry. I should have known.'

'Naw, it ain't like that,' Ed reassured her. 'We got separated in a fight. Got themselves trapped in a cave. Had them bears closing in on me, I couldn't hang around. Had to bail out.'

Sophie panicked, 'They're in a cave?' She remembered everything that Daniels had said, about the underground detonation, the fusion of the tectonic plates, the containment of the blast under the surface. 'There's a nuclear bomb,' she blurted out. 'They've set it to go off underground. If we don't stop it, it'll nuke this whole park.' Ed scoffed, but Sophie pressed him. 'Even if we survive on the surface, anyone in a cave will be as good as dead.'

He stopped. Ed thought of Brad and Dennis. Of the old couple who saved him from that first attack. Of the kids, the one who saved his life by blowing up the RV...

Ed looked to the bomb casing in the distance. It stood undisturbed.

'I take it that's it?' he asked.

Sophie nodded. 'Can you help us?'

Ed took a sharp intake of breath, like a mechanic trying to upsell some engine repairs. 'Today's your lucky day, sweetheart. Saw me some action in Iraq.' He pronounced it *Eye-Rack*. 'You got yourself a bonafide 'munitions expert right here.' He puffed out his chest, proudly.

'Cool! Let's get that timer stopped!' Tyler shouted.

Ed reigned Tyler in. 'Now hold up there small fry. Case you din't notice, this whole area be crawling with critters. You expect they just let us walk on over there and say 'Hi'?' He shook his head and gave the matter some thought. 'We need us a distraction.'

'What do you suggest?' Sophie asked.

He looked around, his eyes settling on Tyler. He reached for his pocket, checking he still had some ammunition left.

Tyler looked confused.

There was a twinkle in Ed's eye. 'Your papa ever teach you how to use a grenade, boy?'

Tyler suspected there wasn't much call for that sort of thing in accounting.

Kevin peered over the edge of the roof.

The bears continued to amass underneath them. A couple fought over the mangled remains of the Mayor. The rest hunted for scraps, whilst one or two had a mind to climb the Ranger Station and get to Kevin and Carly.

'What do we do now?' Carly asked, numbly.

Kevin weighed up his options.

By all accounts, the army had been ambushed. He couldn't say for sure if the bomb had been loaded in to position. If it had, then they could repair the tectonic plates. If not, they were about to be wiped out.

There was no more rescue parties.

So the options seemed to be; death by nuclear explosion, or death by bear.

He opted not to vocalise this to Carly.

'We need to get out,' he pondered, 'If we can reach a car, or attract a rescue helicopter.' He had no idea how he was going to do either of those things.

He looked to the parking lot below.

The Sheriff's old Pontiac sat undisturbed. If only he could reach it. It was a tough old car, he might be able to force his way through. Once he hit the road, he'd be on his way. He could get help.

Crossing to the corner nearest to the car, he looked for a means of escape. There was a telegraph pole beyond the parking lot. The wire ran right over the Pontiac. He could zip line down to it.

Would it hold his weight? The wire only stretched as far as the corner of the building. He'd have to dangle himself off the roof in plain sight of all these bears and hope he could get to the car before they reached him.

Then he'd have to hotwire it.

He could hotwire a car.

Possibly...

'I'm going for help,' he said, determined.

Carly cried, 'Wait. I want to go. Don't leave me up here.'

He wanted to take Carly with him, but there was no way he would have time for two people to make it to the car. Besides, he couldn't put any more people in danger. After what happened with Sophie...

...and there was the Mayor...

He held his stomach.

'I'll come right back. I promise,' he reassured Carly.

Then, he took his shirt off and lowered himself on to the edge of the roof. He sat with his feet dangling over the side and looked down at the large bears amassing below.

One of them turned its nostrils upward, sniffing at the air.

A scent.

Fresh meat sat just out of reach. It snorted, hungrily, then stood on its hind legs trying to reach the Deputy.

He panicked, his breathing quickened. He watched as the other bears started to realise that there was a meal hanging tantalisingly out of reach. He knew that if he didn't move now, the space below would be so deep in bears that he's never make it to the car.

Kevin wrapped his shirt around the telegraph wire. It was attached at the guttering and ran down to the telephone lines at the reception desk. The guttering creaked under his weight.

He ran his shirt up and down the wire a few times, testing its traction.

This might just work.

Closing his eyes, he tensed his arms.

Carly shouted, but it was too late. Deputy Kevin shuffled off the roof, his arms tensing, the wire bending downwards, his shirt sliding. He held his feet up, trying to keep out of reach of the bears, their claws dangerously close.

But it was working.

The makeshift zipwire was speeding him towards Hank's Pontiac.

The bears were left reeling. Furious that their meal was escaping. The roared in frustration.

Looking down, his feet had cleared the bears. He was now above the parking lot. In a few seconds, he would be at the car.

There was a sound.

He thought it was the telegraph wire at first, but it was louder and more immediate.

Then he jolted.

The shirt was tearing.

Before he had chance to think, there was a loud rip and the shirt split in half. He immediately lost all forward momentum and started to fall. His arms waved frantically, the two halves of shirt still clenched in his fists.

He could hear Carly yelp in terror as she watched.

Then there was a thud and a loud crack as Deputy Kevin hit the tarmac. At first, he was relieved – he'd fallen short, but at least he had landed safely. But when he tried to stand, a pain shot through his leg.

It was fractured.

The bears turned towards him, their prey sat prone on the tarmac.

In an adjacent tunnel, Brad and Saul had located an old mine cart. Saul had been concerned that any cart they found at this stage would be too rusted to move, but it had been preserved in near perfect condition.

Which meant his plan would go ahead.

He didn't know whether he was relieved or disappointed.

Instead, he put his mind to moving it. And beside the much younger Brad, he was determined to show that he still had what it took when it came to heavy lifting. The two of them managed to get the cart rolling and it wasn't long before it rolled on through to the junction at which Rita and Aimee stood.

He shouted for them to man the switch. Aimee threw all her weight behind the lever and managed to align the track with the tunnel that led back to the bear den.

Saul and Brad took a breath, the sweat now pouring down Saul's back. He leaned gasping against the wall from the exertion. 'It's heavier than I thought.'

'Probably not been used in a hundred years,' Brad was also out of breath. 'We're lucky it moves at all.'

Aimee looked angry. She chastised Brad, 'You're serious about this.'

He didn't look Aimee in the eye. Saul watched silently. He was inclined to agree with Aimee. Brad was offering to throw his life away to bring a stop to those things. Saul wondered when was the best time to talk to Brad, but he caught sight of his wife – how would he tell her...?

'If this is about Dennis...' Aimee continued.

'This is about stopping these things from escaping.' Brad was frustrated and Saul got the impression that he expected everyone to understand the sacrifice – even after everything that had happened today.

Aimee tried pleading, 'We could go for help, get the Army to...'

Brad cut her off, 'There's no time. We woke that den up trying to get across. We have to finish this.' And then turned away, opening the rucksack and preparing the dynamite. He started tying the small fuse wires together, trying to ensure an even distribution from the one light.

It was all they would get. One chance.

Aimee then approached Saul, angrily, 'Are you okay with this?'

Saul didn't want to argue. Not any more. Not ever again. 'I tried talking to him, Aimee. What happens here, it has to happen this way. Please understand that.' She was furious. He continued, 'You're a good kid. I wish I could have met you under better circumstances.'

'We'll get out. We'll escape.'

But Saul no longer had an intention of escaping. His response was non committal. Instead, he gave Aimee a hug. Holding her tight, he whispered in to her ear;

'Look after Rita for me.'

As he pulled away, he could see the realisation across Aimee's face. He had made his intention clear to Brad as they hunted for the mine cart, had asked that he not tell the girls anything.

But it was time.

He gazed lovingly at his wife and tried to keep himself composed. Aimee had backed away, knowing that it was too late to convince him otherwise.

Brad finished loading the dynamite. He approached Saul and gave him instructions as Saul readied himself for what he needed to do. But Saul couldn't tear his eyes away from his wife, who stood there innocent to events. Brad handed Saul his lighter.

'The fuses are linked, but they're short. Just light the end and it should ignite them all.'

Saul nodded.

And suddenly, his wife realised his plan.

'Saul?' Rita rushed to him, panicked, 'Saul, you can't...'

He held her hands, 'I'm sorry Rita, my love. I have to.'

'But it was Brad. He...'

Saul spoke softly, 'Brad is a young man who has just lost all of his friends. He needs to go home. Me, I'm just some old, retired shmuck. I've lived my life.' He smiled at her, a single tear ran down his cheek. 'I love you, Rita. I've loved every moment of our fifty years together.'

Rita wept, 'You can't do this, Saul. It's so...'

'Selfish?' Saul squeezed her, 'That's what this trip was for, wasn't it? For us to start thinking about each other and not worry about other people. Well, let me have this last self indulgence - making sure you're safe.'

Saul blinked away his tears as Rita sobbed.

They held each other for the last time.

'I love you.'

'Goodbye, my sweetheart. Look after the grandchildren for me.'

They shared one last lingering kiss and stared deep in to each other's eyes. Saul knew what came next, but he wished he could just close his eyes now and never reopen them. If that was his last moment with Rita, his life was already over.

He looked to Brad, who took Rita by the shoulders and led her away.

Aimee hesitated. 'Saul, I don't know what to say.'

'Nick was a lovely fella, Aimee,' Saul offered. 'He saved us all. Time for me to return the favour.'

She hugged him, then turned away speechless.

Saul nodded to Brad, who gave Aimee and the sobbing Rita the word.

They started to run.

He waited for their footsteps to fade, then leaned against the minecart. He wiped the tears from his eyes and sighed.

'Well Saul, it's just you and the Bears now.'

CHAPTER 16

Lori had slowly started to back away, followed by Hank. The closer the magma bear came, the deeper they retreated in to the shadows. But the bears attention was entirely focused on Avon.

Quietly, they climbed in to a small alcove and watched.

Avon's chanting became louder, more intense. He stood on the dais, eyes closed. Lori couldn't tell if he knew the bear was approaching or not and she felt a well of fear for him.

The bear was so close to Avon. One swipe of its paw and he was dead. But it seemed reasonably calm for the moment, although still menacing and completely terrifying.

The furious chanting was certainly irritating the creature and Lori twitched.

'We need to warn him.'

Could she warn him? Avon's mind seemed so far away. There would be no guarantee that he would listen to anything she might say. Still, she had to try. She went to move from her hiding place, but Hank held her back.

'He knows what he's doing.'

'That bear will kill him,' Lori whispered, nervously.

But Hank had faith. He indicated to the dais. 'Just let this play out.'

The bear was circling the dais, watching Avon intently. It bared its huge teeth as it stalked him. Hank was fascinated.

'You see that? It's studying him.'

Lori thought back to the ambush at the waterfall. The bears were so coordinated. Avon was certain they had led them there, but Lori wasn't totally convinced. 'You don't think it's...'

'I don't know,' Hank silenced her.

Now there was more noise. Further grunting and scraping from adjoining chambers. Just as the bear had emerged from the darkness, more shapes began to enter the room. Several more magma bears, as large and as menacing as the first. Lori gasped. She wondered how they planned to escape if all this failed.

Snarling, they took up positions surrounding the dais.

'We fear your wrath, All Mother.
We feel your fury and we tremble.
We ask now for your forgiveness,
so that we may learn from the mistakes
of our ancestors. Forgive us, All Mother,
that we might change!'

Avon shouted his prayer to the heavens and the bears watched him, growling their deep, guttural yearning for flesh. They started edging closer and closer to the dais.

Lori was increasingly anxious. They were going to kill him.

There was another rumble. Not an earthquake, more like a train roaring past. It was a force – a power flowing unseen through the Temple.

The All Mother was watching.

Ed lifted a pair of binoculars from the valley floor. There was something attached to them. He batted it away.

It was a hand.

Sophie flinched as the limb bounced in to the gravel. She avoided Ed's gaze, sensing his stupid grin.

He scanned the valley through the binoculars. Sophie shielded her eyes from the fading sunlight as she followed his gaze. On the other side of the geyser, a scrawny arm waved.

It was Tyler. He had made it.

'That's the signal,' Ed confirmed. 'The lamb is in position.'

'Don't call him that.'

Ed shrugged flippantly, 'Why not? Can't make an omelette without breaking some eggs.'

She raised her fist, ready to chastise Ed, when suddenly there was a deep rumble in the earth. It seemed to pass by them and continue in to the distance. She thought it was heading towards the cliffs in the distance.

'What the hell was that?' Sophie wondered.

Ed looked confused. 'The grenade?'

Sophie knew it wasn't. But she noticed an interesting effect. The bears ears pricked up. They stopped feasting on their carcasses and they listened intently. Their heads all turned collectively in the direction that Sophie had followed – the cliffs.

'Look at them,' she prompted Ed, who then watched the bears.

They all stood up on their hind legs, completely attentive. They were listening. Watching.

Something was alarming them.

What could possibly perturb a magma bear?

'They got the scent of something, for sure,' Ed surmised. 'Time to start launching them grenades.'

Before he could give Tyler the signal, Sophie stopped him. 'No, wait.'

Slowly, the bears started to move off towards the rumbling.

They were leaving. Drawn to the sound.

Their slow stride then picked up pace and they began to run away from the geyser towards some unidentified threat.

'What's got them so distracted?' Sophie was surprised.

Ed was far more pragmatic. 'Who cares? Go.' And he ran across the valley, Sophie giving chase. From the opposite side of the geyser, Tyler saw them break from cover and sprinted out to join them.

Meanwhile, the bomb continued its count down.

They were within reach of it now. A thin gantry hung across the scaffold that held the bomb in position.

Sophie followed behind Ed as he raced up the small metal steps. The gantry rocked as they crossed towards the access panel.

Ed stopped and considered the mechanisms. Then with brute force, tore the panel away. It came free easily, exposing some wiring behind.

She peered over his shoulder. It was like every movie she had ever seen. A red wire, a blue and a yellow.

Which did you cut?

The blue? It was always the blue in the movies...

Ed grimaced. 'God damn.'

'Can you stop it?' she asked.

He reached his hand deeper in to the casing, feeling around, 'No. There's no way to stop it.'

Sophie's heart stopped. This was it.

Tyler twitched beside her. 'Then what are you waiting for? We need to run!'

Ed was nervous. He had started to sweat. 'Now hold on there, Flash. I can't disarm this thing, but I can sure as Hell stop it going nuclear.'

There was a glimmer of hope. Sophie breathed.

'How?' she asked.

He continued to fidget with the internal mechanism, 'These things, they're just basic explosives with a separate warhead rigged inside 'em.' He paused as he yanked at a few wires. 'Remove the nuclear warhead, it ain't a nuke anymore. Just a regular ol' bomb.'

There was a clunk.

The nose cone of the bomb casing – pointing down toward the geyser – came loose. Ed reached down below the gantry, grunting as he tried to pull the cone up on to the platform. Sophie and Tyler helped.

They dragged it up alongside them. Ed opened another compartment.

Inside was a metal rod.

Sophie was unimpressed. 'Is that it?'

'Yup.'

His hands trembled as he worked intently on freeing it from the casing. Beads of sweat ran down his face with the intense concentration. Sophie watched the veins pop out across his temples, his face flushed. She glanced at the timer.

The numbers continued to tick away.

Ed winced as he jolted the small nuclear rod in its container, desperate not to shock it too much.

But the jolt knocked it free.

Ed lifted it from the casing. Slowly, he turned to Tyler, handing him the charge. 'Hold this for me, Chief.'

'What is it?' Tyler almost tossed it from hand to hand, but Ed stopped him.

'Plutonium. Try not to drop it, y'hear?'

Tyler backed away, cradling the plutonium like a newborn infant.

With half of the job completed, Ed turned back to the timer. The three wires that Sophie had noticed initially.

'I can't jam the guidance,' he said, frustrated.

'Meaning?'

'Meaning this here bomb ain't nuclear, but it could still take out my friends.'

Sophie remembered – Ed had friends hiding out in the caves. An underground blast could still trap them, or worse. But the timer continued to count down.

'Tyler, you need to get out of here. Get that as far away from here as possible,' Sophie instructed. Tyler turned and ran down the steps, being extra careful with the nuclear charge in his hands. She watched as he headed for the trees, then turned back to Ed. He looked intense.'

'You've diffused the nuke. Let's go,' she shouted.

'Not until I've stopped this goddamn thing from exploding,' he snarled.

'You said you can't stop the guidance. It'll launch in to the geyser and take you with it.'

'Not if I pull the trigger first.'

Sophie stopped, her eyes widened. She had hated Ed this morning, but now...

He shouted, 'Why you still here, girl? Didn't I tell you to go on?'

Sophie backed away, words failing her. She watched how intently he was working, struggling desperately to prevent further harm to friends who may be affected by an underground explosion.

This man who was just another heartless hunter to her this morning.

'I said *GO!*' he barked.

She ran, not looking back, not stopping.

Sophie ran for her life.

Deputy Kevin scrambled up on to his good leg. He tried to put pressure on the fractured leg – an intense pain shot through it. But it was nothing compared to what would happen if those bears caught him.

They turned towards him, smelling the flesh from his open wound.

He limped on, the Pontiac mere feet away.

From the rooftop, Carly tried to cause distraction. She pounded against the side of the building. A few bears bought the distraction. They turned towards her and started trying to climb the build. The roof shook from the weight of the bears against it.

Deputy Kevin dragged himself further. The bears were faster. They were closing the gap between them and him. They were so close now he could smell them.

He lunged at the car, falling against it. He had made it.

Now all he had to do was...

He tried the door.

He tried again.

This was the worst rescue plan in history.

Deputy Kevin turned to face the magma bears.

Ahead, Aimee saw something she never thought she would see again. There was a faint glimmer of daylight and she could feel the touch of a soft breeze against her skin. They were almost free. She prayed nothing waited for her on the outside.

Brad brought up the rear, dragging Rita screaming. She was trying to turn back, but it was no use. The die had been cast. She thought she could hear the murmur of bears further down the tunnel. They must be almost on top of

Saul by now.

She ran. Harder. Faster.

They couldn't risk another cave in.

They needed to get through that tunnel before the blast.

Saul sat perched upon the mine cart, the picture of serenity. It was time. His casual acceptance of this surprised even him. But his wife was in danger. He did what he had to do.

Playfully, he flicked the lighter in his hand.

He heard the approaching growl, the bears were close now. He reached for the fuse, making sure it was to hand. He was surprised to see he was shaking. Saul steadied himself and waited.

A wave of fiery red eyes stared back at him from the tunnel.

They had arrived.

Saul grinned at the magma bears as they slowly stepped from the shadows.

'There you are. I've been waiting for you,' he told them. They watched him, hungrily. Their first meal since hibernation. He continued; 'Tried to push this cart, but my back's not what it used to be.'

The nearest bear growled at him. He ignored it.

'You hear the story of Goldilocks and the Three Bears?'

He paused.

'Looks like we'll all be sleeping in the same bed.'

Saul flicked open the lighter.

It didn't spark.

Saul almost swore.

The nearest bear jumped on him. Saul grabbed for the dynamite, gripping the fuse tightly in his fist. The lighter dropped to the floor out of reach.

The magma bear stood over him, drooling in his face, toying with its food. The eyes were burning red. He saw the orange veins popping under the rocky hide. These things truly were born of fire.

He held the fuse up to the melting hot skin of the bear.

A claw sank in to his abdomen. The pain was unbearable.

Just another second more.

Some smoke.

The other bears surrounded the mine cart, their noses pushing in to the makeshift trough, chewing at his limbs. He stifled a scream.

The fuse caught.

Sparks raced down the wire.

The weeds and branches that hung over the exit camouflaged the tunnel perfectly. It was no wonder it lay undisturbed for so long. Any tracks or paths leading from the mouth of the tunnel down the hill had been lost to time.

That was until Aimee burst through the overgrowth at breakneck speed, followed immediately by Brad and Rita.

Aimee tumbled, crashing headfirst down the hillside, rolling all the way down. Brad threw Rita behind a tree – sufficient cover, he hoped.

They all paused, expectantly, then...

- *BOOM* -

A fireball licked out from the tunnel, singeing the branches of the trees. The rocks began to crumble. Aimee watched as the earth gave way and a small landslide of soil and rubble sealed the cave entrance off permanently.

Aimee breathed.

Rita rolled over, screaming in torment, 'Saul! *SAUL!*'

But he was gone. Their nightmare was almost over.

CHAPTER 17

A large paw stepped up on to the dais as the bears closed in around Avon, the saliva frothing at their mouths. The room grew smaller and smaller as more bears arrived, filling every available space, clambering over each other from outside the chamber.

They were ready for the kill.

But Avon was unmoved. He continued to pray, alternating between English and a chant in his native language.

Lori felt completely helpless. 'They'll kill him.'

'He's got them,' Hank whispered beside her. 'Whatever it is that he's doing, it's working. You can't stop him now.'

'We have to distract them,' she suggested.

Hank waved her off, 'No, wait. He has this. Trust me.'

Lori couldn't tear her eyes away. She almost let out a cry as the largest amongst the bears jumped up on to the dais and lunged at Avon, unexpectedly. It caught Avon off guard and he broke away from his prayer, eyes open just in time to see how close the predator was.

He flinched, staggering backwards, arms up in protection.

The bear lunged again.

From the corner of her eye, Lori saw another bear, bounding across the backs of those that surrounded the dais, lighter of foot than they.

She recognised this bear. Not a magma bear.

It was Spirit.

He crashed in to the bear that threatened Avon, knocking it down on to the dais, narrowly avoiding Avon who stepped to one side helpless.

The magma bears saw their opening.

They started jumping up on to the dais themselves, entering the fray. But Spirit placed himself between Avon and his attackers, snarling and biting at any magma bear that advanced.

Spurned on by the sacrifice of his friend, Avon continued his prayer. This only made the magma bears angry. They attacked, Spirit desperately fending them off valiantly.

The magma bears were twice Spirit's size. Spurned on by their anger, they tore at the grizzly, tossing him aside like a rag doll.

Avon looked down as his companion crashed to the ground at his feet, defeated.

The magma bears regrouped, rid of their distraction.

They roared. The chamber echoed with rage.

But Avon no longer saw his attackers. His safety

was no longer his concern. Instead, he dropped to his knees before Spirit in mourning, crying out his name.

Lori felt Hank shift beside her. He had decided this was enough.

He jumped from their hiding place, waving his arms to cause a distraction. He shouted his friend, 'Avon, you have to run! They'll kill you.'

But Avon couldn't hear Hank. Instead, he cradled the dying bear in his arms and stroked its face. 'Spirit, my dear friend. You saved me. You saved my life.' He held him close, the two companions face to face for their final moments together. Lori thought back to their initial conversation about Spirit – how Avon expected one day he may turn on him, that it was in the bears nature. Today, nothing could be further from the truth.

Avon's eyes welled with tears. They began to cascade down his face, gathering at his chin.

They dripped on to the fur of Spirit.

Lori was reminded of the scene from Avon's fable – his Great Grandfather weeping over the death of a fallen bear...

And suddenly, a tremendous light emanated from Avon's fallen friend.

Warm.

Glowing.

It then spread out, a shockwave from the centre of the Temple, emanating from Spirit on the dais, passing through all that it touched, seemingly harmless. Lori felt its warmth as it washed over her and she was overwhelmed by a feeling.

Forgiveness.

The magma bears stopped. Their fur stiffened and creaked.

Suddenly, a great groan erupted from the Temple.

Hank and Lori stepped forward, fascinated. Lori approached the bears, Hank trying to hold her back, but she needed to see. She needed to reach out and touch this, to prove it was real.

The bears started to fall, one by one, collapsing to the ground and crumbling apart, turning to dust before their eyes, returning to the volcanic rubble from whence they came.

Lori prodded one of the magma bears. Its skin was solid. It crumpled under the weight of her touch.

Deputy Kevin sank down beside the old Pontiac. He could see the Ranger Station buckling behind the bears. Soon they would reach Carly and kill her too. How could he have been so stupid.

He closed his eyes and waited for death.

The magma bears loomed over him.

And stopped.

They creaked to a halt, frozen. Then they turned to dust.

Ed stood alone in an empty valley, fishing through wires and circuitry inside the bomb casing. He had a pocket knife in his hand, and waved it around as he traced the origins of each respective wire. Beads of sweat ran down his face.

The timer to launch was almost out.

He sighed, defeated and dropped his arms, limply.

'Aw, to Hell with this.'

He tightened the wires in his hand and brought the knife up behind them. Without a further thought, he sliced right through them all indiscriminately.

The circuit broke.

The bomb exploded. In the brief second before it hit him, Ed felt relief – relief that the nuclear charge was far away, relief that Dennis and Brad would be safe.

What was one less redneck in a national park, anyways?

The blast engulfed him.

Hank crouched down, reaching out towards a pile of ash on the floor. What the hell had he just witnessed? Quietly, he ran his hand through the ashes and let it flow through his fingers.

It was real. He didn't know what it was, but it was real.

He watched Lori, who stood over Avon. She tried to comfort him as he cradled his fallen spirit guide. Avon had barely looked up since Spirit's death. It was as if nothing else mattered. Hank didn't pretend to understand that bond. He doubted he ever could.

Avon cried, 'He saved us all.'

'*You* saved us all,' Lori corrected him, 'The All Mother saw your sacrifice. She forgave.'

Hank approached the dais, the dust from the magma bears kicked up in to the air as he walked. The room was thick with dust. He offered a hand to Avon.

Avon looked up at the Sheriff. An unspoken bond passed between them as they shared a knowing glance. Avon took Hank's outstretched hand and he was pulled to his feet. Hank beamed at him, proudly.

'You did it.'

Avon's eyes cleared. He saw the dusty room for the first time and gasped with delight. He embraced his cynical old friend, 'Not bad for a crazy old man.'

Hank simply laughed and added sincerely, 'Never doubted you for a second.'

Together, they left the chamber. It was time to go home.

CHAPTER 18

By the time the emergency services arrived, the dust from the fallen magma bears had scattered in the wind. Deputy Kevin collapsed in to a heap on the steps of the Ranger Station. The floor boards were shattered, the cabin itself on a slight angle. The windows and doors were destroyed.

Ambulances littered the parking lot, tending to any injured that they could find. Kevin was pleased to see a few Rangers stagger back through the trees, sharing stories of attempted rescues, of hiding in trees and narrow escapes. It was good to know he and Carly weren't the only survivors.

Shortly after, two teenagers staggered down the path towards them. Carly raced towards them, embracing them. Kevin watched them and smiled.

Sophie was safe.

A Police Officer took a small device from Tyler, who breathed a sigh of relief.

Sat at the door of one of the ambulances, Kevin could see a young girl and an elderly woman. The girl comforted the woman who, apart from a few scrapes, looked unharmed. He wondered at what they had gone through. How many bodies were out there in the park, awaiting someone to come and clean them up? He supposed they may never recover everyone.

And Kevin thought of Hank and Lori.

It felt like a lifetime since he had seen the Sheriff. They had gone to the geyser, which he figured was the source of all this destruction. He was anxious for Sophie, who he could see surveying the crowd looking for her father.

A paramedic approached Kevin and tried to tend to his fractured leg, but he waved them off as Sophie came running over.

She looked to Kevin, hoping for news.

His eyes were heavy. He just shook his head and Sophie wept. He tried to stand up, to comfort her, but he fell back down – his leg now completely numb.

Kevin heard an approaching engine. The ambulances and fire crews had raced off in to the park in search of the seriously injured. He presumed some were now returning.

But it wasn't an emergency vehicle.

Hank's Jeep drove slowly through the carnage. The door swung open and Hank jumped out, unharmed.

Frantically, Hank searched through the wounded and Kevin waved his arms. 'Hank? Hank!'

Sophie looked up, her eyes locked with Hank and they both raced towards each other. Lori and Avon watched from the Jeep as they shared a long embrace. Hank was crying. He wiped the tears away as he pulled away and checked his daughter.

'Are you unhurt? Let me look at you.'

'Dad, I'm fine. I'm fine.'

He squeezed her tight, a smile beaming from his face. He looked back to Avon, who gave him a proud nod.

Hank put his arm around his daughter's shoulder and they walked towards his car.

'So,' he asked her, 'you still against Bear Hunting Season?'

Sophie shrugged. 'I dunno, Dad. I guess some bears just gotta go.'

Epilogue

700 Years Ago

The sun reached its lowest point in the Arctic sky. At this time of year, it was endless day. But he knew that the low sun signified night. It was time to head home to his family.

His shadow was long beside him at the fishing hole, reaching as far as his sled. The dogs sat beside it, waiting patiently for their master to finish the hunt. He stood, packing away his spear and wrapping the fish in skins to preserve them for the journey.

The snow crunched under his feet as he approached the sled. The dogs yapped, expectantly. He climbed aboard and with a whip of the reigns, the dogs sprung in to action.

Contentedly, the fisherman sped towards his village. He could see it against the horizon, a small group of igloos, built from whalebone and hides and insulated with thickly compacted snow. As he drew closer, he could make out a small campfire. The villagers sat around it, waiting the return of their tribesmen.

His friends greeted him heartily as his sled came to a halt. He climbed down and shared a joke with a fellow fisherman as two children ran from his home to greet him. He gave them both a great hug. His wife stood in the doorway, smiling.

Sat at a small fire, he stripped from his furs and warmed himself as his wife prepared the fresh fish he had caught. They ate as a family. With their bellies full, the children went off to bed and he soon joined them. Tomorrow, he would rise early and travel out to the next village. He had heard of an abundance of seal in the area and he hoped to help with the hunt.

He drifted in to a peaceful sleep.

A few hours passed before his eyes opened, fully alert. He heard the crunch of approaching pawprints.

Slowly, he got to his feet and peered through the doorway.

He froze.

The crisp white snow had been washed red with blood.

They had come for the villagers.

Quietly, he roused his family, urging the children not to panic. His wife shushed them as they quickly dressed and stood ready at the door.

Their way seemed clear.

He told them to make for the sled. They were not to stop, not to look around. They must do exactly as he tells them.

The children nodded.

He kissed them on the forehead, then nodded to

his wife.

Go.

They ran.

Exactly as he told them, they headed straight for the sled. He followed behind, making sure no one fell behind. And he turned to the village, to take one last look at his home.

Two of them stood there, staring back at him, their skin like glass, a blue fire raging within. Their faces were stained with blood and he realised that they were stood over the bodies of the villagers, feasting.

They both roared at him, then stepped forward, their razor-ice claws scraping the snow as they moved.

He ran.

THE HORROR CONTINUES
IN
POLAR BEARQUAKE

ABOUT THE AUTIIOR

David Griffiths is an author, screenwriter and playwright from Liverpool, England. He has written comics for *FUTURE QUAKE* and *ZARJAZ* and his latest comic (with artist Jon Lon) is *MAELSTROM*. His Dickensian Christmas parody, *A CHRISTMAS CTHULHU* debuted on Amazon's Top 10 New Horror and is available in Paperback and on Kindle.

When he's not writing, David is the producer and co-founder of the British American Sports Network, commentating on local ice hockey games for popular TV series *DROP THE PUCK*. His critically acclaimed sports documentary series, *DRAGONS' FIRE* is available on YouTube.

Follow David on Twitter
@daveygriff82

Printed in Great Britain
by Amazon

54564730R00135